Midsummer Nights

Secrets of Mackinac Island

Katie Winters

Chapter One

Cindy and Tracey Swartz crept along a Mackinac Island sailing dock, their feet bare against the harsh wood. Before them, a soft pink sunrise swelled along the horizon. They'd just returned from a four-mile run, their legs stretched out as they silently crept along, welcoming the brand-new day with open arms.

"Are you sure about this?" Cindy whispered, turning to look at Tracey.

"Am I ever sure about anything?" Tracey asked, a soft smile creeping toward her ear.

"You're always sure. It's the 'being right' thing that you're not so good at," Cindy muttered back, chuckling softly.

Tracey's heart surged in her chest, transparent with hope. It was the first day of summer— June 21 and around them, Mackinac Island had sprung to life, its lilacs screaming with purple blooms, its trees dewy and green. With a spontaneous rush of adrenaline, she pulled off her running shirt and shorts and stood in only her sports bra and underwear. Cindy followed suit.

"If anyone sees us out here..." Cindy began.

"What?" Tracey asked, hands on her hips, a look of defiance marring her face. "What are they going to do?"

"It's not every day that two forty-something women go skinny-dipping."

"Forty-something?" Tracey tossed her hands in the air with exaggeration and eyed her elder sister. "What did we say about being ageist toward ourselves? Besides. This is my last morning on the island for a while."

"Like ten days," Cindy pointed out.

"Ten days! Off the island! Do you remember the last time you spent ten days off the island, Cindy?" Tracey demanded. "Celebrate this next part of my life with me, won't you?"

"Does it have to be this way?" Cindy asked, cocking her head.

Oh, but Tracey knew that Cindy couldn't deny how delicious the water looked. It lapped coolly against the side of the docks and tipped the sailboats into one another.

"I'm going in, whether you want to or not," Tracey shot out. "But know that I'll remember this moment as the time my older sister let me down."

Cindy groaned. As Tracey swung her sports bra over her shoulders and smacked it across the dock, Cindy cried, "Okay, okay. I'll do it."

Tracey waited with bated breath as her older sister got completely undressed. She felt like a teenager again, long before their tremendous heartache— before Cindy's boyfriend, Jeremy, passed away; before Tracey had learned she was accidentally pregnant; before their mother had died.

After a moment of silence, they latched hands and locked eyes.

"One."

"Two."

"Three!"

Together, they leaped from the dock, their limbs flailing just before they crashed into the pink-tinged waves. Tracey collapsed deep beneath the blue, her eyes closed. Lake water threatened to fill her nose, but she breathed out as hard as she could. Bubbles pummelled to the surface.

The water felt so fresh against her sweaty skin. Beneath the water, the weight of her limbs and the aching of her joints retreated. It was just Tracey, as she'd always been— renewed through the nourishing beauty of a Mackinac summertime.

Tracey erupted from the surface, whipping her hair back. Around her, the water remained quiet, frothing against the dock.

"Cindy?" Tracey called. Her voice echoed across the sailboats and surrounding docks. "Hey, Cindy? Where are you?" Tracey's heartbeat escalated. Fear mounted. Why hadn't her sister come to the surface yet? Where on earth could she be?

"I'm here." Cindy half-wailed from the dock, where she hid behind a thick wooden log. She grimaced with her arms wrapped around the log. "I thought I saw someone walking on the dock and totally panicked."

Tracey cackled. "You're a chicken."

"You can call me whatever you want."

"Feels pretty good, though. Doesn't it?" Tracey asked. She combed her fingers through her hair, her grin widening. "Nothing better than a sunrise swim after a run."

Cindy grimaced. "How am I going to get out without the entire island seeing me? Oh, this was stupid. This was so stupid. I can't believe I let you talk me into this."

Tracey groaned and frog-kicked her legs to swim closer to the dock. As she prepared a plan to get Cindy out of the water without being noticed, a voice rose out from the docks.

"What on earth has gotten into you girls?"

Cindy's eyes widened in shock at the first sound. She looked just as frightened as she had back in elementary school when she'd decided to sneak the pet hamster into class to show off to her friends. (Tracey still teased Cindy about this, as it was one of Cindy's finest acts of recklessness. Naturally, Cindy had gotten into heaps of trouble at the time.)

"Hello?" Tracey called back, unafraid.

A woman in her fifties, wearing running pants and a tank top, crept along the dock, peering out across the water.

"Marcy! What the heck are you doing around here so early?" Tracey's heart lifted at the sight of the long-time bartender at the Pink Pony, a woman who knew the ins and outs of all island gossip.

"You think I keep this figure just pouring beer and liquor at the bar?" Marcy shot back. "I'm up and ready to go every morning at five. Planning on a six-miler this morning."

"You're Wonder Woman, Marcy," Tracey called, cackling. "You want to join my sister and I for a swim?"

Cindy swatted the water toward Tracey, clearly annoyed that Tracey had given Cindy's name away.

"Don't you worry yourself, Cindy," Marcy said, clucking her tongue. "It's nothing I haven't seen before, let me tell you."

Tracey's stomach seized with laughter. Cindy looked absolutely mortified. With an exasperated sigh, Tracey finally said, "Marcy? Could you do us a favor, please?"

"I suppose that you girls think that I'm always at your beck and call," Marcy replied. "But as you can see, I'm not behind the bar right now."

"Marcy! After everything we've been through? You won't help us out?" Cindy demanded.

Marcy tapped her chin with a delicate finger. "All right. I'll hear you out. What do you need?"

"Cindy's a bit nervous about the public seeing her in this sensitive position," Tracey explained. "Could you shield her as she gets her clothes back on?"

"Never should have gone along with this," Cindy groaned.

Marcy was clearly enjoying herself. She paused for a moment, pretending to give this some real thought. After a dramatic pause, she turned and spread her arms out wide, blocking off a bit of space for Cindy to leap up and hide behind her. With rushed motions, she draped herself with her running clothes and then stood, panting. Water trickled from her hair.

But after a split second, Cindy locked eyes with Tracey again, and the two sisters howled with laughter. Marcy leaped away from Cindy, her tank top sopping wet at the bottom. Quickly, Tracey joined her sister on the dock, taking her time to get herself back into her t-shirt.

"Cindy, there's nobody around," Tracey said, gesturing out across the empty walkway toward Fort Mackinac and the Island House Hotel. "It's a ghost town."

Cindy grumbled. "Marcy was around."

"And I'm glad I was," Marcy said, her voice laced with sarcasm. "You've given me something to laugh about. That's about all this old lady needs to get through the day."

"Marcy, you do know you're only about seven or eight years older than me, right?" Cindy asked mischievously.

Marcy waved a hand. "Don't you give me that. I watched you grow up from that bar counter." She then turned back to catch both Tracey and Cindy's eyes. Hers glittered knowingly. "I know that you've both been through a great deal over the years. Seeing you leap off that dock this morning... It reminded me that we're all just kids who had to pretend to grow up."

And with that, Marcy lifted her tennis shoes and bounded down the dock, beginning her six-mile run. She left Tracey and Cindy drenched with lake water, their hearts pumping with gladness.

It would be a gorgeous summer.

Chapter Two

The screen door screeched open. Tracey froze over the top of her suitcase, still in just a pair of shorts and an oversized t-shirt. Her hair was wrapped in a fluffy bath towel, and the suitcase was only half-filled— proof that she was still far from ready.

"Mom?" There it was, Tracey's daughter, Emma's sweet voice. "Are you here?"

"In here, honey!" Tracey shoved several pairs of underwear into the corner of her suitcase, annoyed with herself. She'd spent the better part of the morning cackling with Cindy on the front porch, talking about the good old times as the lake water had dried from their hair.

Emma stopped in the doorway and giggled. "You haven't finished packing yet?"

Tracey scrunched her nose. "Want to help?"

Emma dropped on the edge of Tracey's bed and eyed the large stack of pants, shirts, and dresses. "We aren't moving to California, Mom. Just visiting."

"I know. I know." Tracey whipped the towel from her hair.

Her hair smacked her back. "But I'm working in costuming, Emma. Fashion! I can't just wander around Los Angeles in a pair of sweatpants and a tank top."

"Not that you ever wear that here," Emma pointed out.

"What did you pack?" Tracey asked, exasperated.

Emma pointed down the hallway, where a medium-sized suitcase sat upright. It was probably a third of the size of Tracey's. Tracey hung her head in shame.

"You're right, though," Emma said, dropping down to lay across her bed. "Megan and I have no plans out in LA besides shopping and lying on the beach. You've got a job to do, and you need the clothes to do it."

Tracey grimaced and lay down beside her daughter, clutching her hand. Her heart beat in double time. She half-considered telling her daughter that her Aunt Cindy had skinny-dipped that morning and been caught by the bartender, Marcy, but soon thought better of it.

"I'm just so nervous that I'm not right for this position," Tracey breathed, mostly to the ceiling.

"Mom. Listen to yourself." Emma popped back up to lock eyes with her mother. "That boutique you've had downtown has been profitable for years, and it's all because of your killer fashion sense. Besides, Elise wouldn't have recommended you for this position if she didn't believe you were right for it. She's in the movie business already."

On the dresser, Tracey's phone began to vibrate. Everything else on the dresser— the hand mirror, the foundation, the creams, shivered along with it. Tracey leaped up to grab it.

"Hi, Elise!" Tracey sounded overly excited, like a teenager on the way to prom.

"Hey there. Penny and I are about to step out the door." Elise sounded as cool as ever. But Elise was only a half-sister, born and raised in Los Angeles. She'd been born cool.

"Oh!" Tracey gaped at her half-filled suitcase. "That should be just fine. Emma and I will meet you on the porch in five minutes."

"Great. And Megan?"

"She'll meet us at the docks," Tracey explained.

Tracey got off the phone as quickly as she could, threw her phone across the bedspread, and began to throw all she could into the rest of her suitcase. She then snapped it closed and sat on the top like she'd seen other stressed women do in movies. Emma laughed and said, "Lift your legs." As Tracey sat on top, Emma slowly zipped the suitcase up.

"Ta-da!" Emma said.

"You're a lifesaver," Tracey replied with an exasperated sigh.

"Do you remember what you packed?" Emma asked.

"Absolutely not."

Emma cackled as Tracey pulled the enormous suitcase from the bed, placing the wheels on the ground first. She tugged it across the carpet and rolled it through the foyer. Just as she reached the doorway, however, Emma called out, "Mom? Aren't you forgetting something?"

Tracey dropped her eyebrows low. "What are you..."

But Emma's smile told her everything she needed to know. With a frustrated groan, Tracey dropped her gaze to her shorts and t-shirt combo, complete with still-damp hair and no makeup.

With that, Tracey flung into action. She buttoned up a light-yellow summer dress, tugged a comb through her hair, moussed it to highlight her curls, and applied foundation, eyeliner, mascara, and a soft coral-colored lipstick. When she emerged from the house seven minutes later, Penny and Elise had only just begun their march up the porch steps.

"Aren't you a sight for sore eyes," Elise said, her arms coming out to wrap Tracey in a hug.

Shepler's Ferry buzzed at the docks expectantly, painted

blue and white with a little cockpit at the top, where the captain sat. A dock worker grabbed their suitcases, tagged them, and placed them on a long rack for safekeeping. When he lifted Tracey's suitcase, he winced with pain.

As Tracey prepared to apologize, however, Elise interjected.

"You're a costume designer, Tracey. It was smart to bring several outfit options. Any other professional would have done the same."

Tracey wasn't entirely sure if this was the truth. Still, she was grateful for the words of comfort and lifted her hand to squeeze Elise's elbow gently. Elise had been a miracle, coming into the lives of the Swartz family at precisely the right time. Tracey still remembered the first time she'd met her at her clothing boutique. At the time, Elise had seemed so frightened, like a fish out of water. Tracey had felt an immediate kinship with her, something that gave her a sense of family. There was no other explanation. A part of her had known she would love her one day.

Tracey sat on the top deck of the ferry. Emma and Megan perched together toward the front, their long hair whipping in the wind. Elise and Penny sat in front of Tracey, chatting about what they planned to eat first in Los Angeles.

"I miss good Asian food," Elise groaned.

"And I miss good bagels!" Penny quipped.

Tracey reached into her purse and grabbed her notebook, which she'd recently purchased as a means to get more organized about her new job. Within, she'd compiled a list of "things to think about" when it came to Mackinac Island fashion in the seventies.

The film itself was based on Elise's screenplay, which she'd written during her first months on the island. Back then, Elise hadn't had a clue who her father was. Through tremendous research, Elise had learned that her mother, Allison Darby, had

had an affair with Tracey's father, Dean, while they both worked for the cinematic masterpiece, *Somewhere in Time*. *Somewhere in Time*, starring Christopher Reeve and Jane Seymour, had been filmed on Mackinac Island back in the late seventies, when Tracey, Cindy, and their very sick little brother, Alex, had been too young to sense their father's extra-marital affair.

It was all in the past, now. If anything, Tracey often felt guilty that Elise had had to grow up without much of a family at all, while Tracey, Cindy, and Alex had had both a mother and a father on the beautiful island of Mackinac.

"Elise, I finished reading the screenplay," Tracey heard herself say, surprising herself.

Elise turned her head. "I'm terrified of what you think."

Tracey's laughter was musical. "I couldn't believe how you brought it all together. You and your mother's story plus the Swartz story. You change from the seventies to the modern times and back again easily, with very emotional results. It's tremendous."

Elise's eyes dampened.

"And the fact that you found a way to honor my mother..." Tracey trailed off, unsure of how to say this.

Elise pressed a hand over Tracey's knee, nodding knowingly. "She was a strong and powerful woman. She slept at Alex's side at the hospital for months. Dean knew he had to stay by her side, while my mother knew that she could go on without him. It's an essential part of the story."

Tracey breathed all the air from her lungs. She felt she'd been punched.

"What's that?" Elise asked, eyeing Tracey's notebook.

"Oh." Tracey laced a strand behind her ear. "I researched a great deal about the island's fashion styles back then."

"Gosh." Elise's lips formed a surprised O. "Donna, the

costume designer, is going to fall in love with you. No doubt in my mind."

"Oh, wow. I'm sure she won't. She'll sense how green I am."

Elise cocked her eyebrow. Her gaze became oddly harsh. "May I say something to you?"

Tracey's voice wavered nervously. "Okay."

"In Hollywood, people believe in one thing and one thing only. Confidence. If you go out there showing them just how little you believe in yourself, they won't believe in you either." Elise swallowed, then added, "You're more qualified than most people in that department. I need you on the team. Keep that in your head. Okay?"

Tracey felt herself nod. "Thank you for saying that."

When Elise turned back to speak to Penny, Tracey eyed the dramatic depths of the Straits of Mackinac. By the end of the day, she'd be out in California, of all places, planning out the next steps of her creative career. It was all beyond her wildest dreams. But no matter how many pep talks Elise gave her, her stomach still twisted with fear.

It would be an interesting journey. That was for sure.

Chapter Three

"Wine. Yes. A glass of wine." Tracey's eyes bugged out as she gripped her armrests. Already, they were tens of thousands of feet in the air, shooting out across the continent and headed toward the west coast. This wasn't normal. This wasn't a boat or a car or a dang horse and buggy.

The stewardess poured Tracey a glass and set it gently on the tray that hung from the back of the chair in front of her. "This should be a really smooth flight," she told Tracey. "Maybe a few bumps over the Rocky Mountains, but nothing major."

"The Rocky Mountains?" Tracey gaped at her.

Emma lifted a finger to catch the stewardess's attention. "Could I have a Diet Coke and some ear plugs? This frightened flier over here is giving me a headache."

Tracey stuck out her tongue as her daughter giggled. The stewardess filled a plastic cup with Diet Coke and passed it over to Emma, who sat by the small window. Tracey resisted peering through that window. The sight of clouds just outside made her stomach twist.

"Oh. And maybe some peanuts?" Emma asked.

"And chocolate," Tracey affirmed.

From behind them, Elise and Penny giggled at Emma and Tracey's madcap ordering.

"Better make that peanut M&Ms," Emma corrected, grabbing her mother's hand, and squeezing like her life depended on it.

"Ow!"

Emma shrugged. "What? I'm nervous, too."

They were island girls through and through. Since Emma's birth, Tracey could count the number of times she'd left the state of Michigan on one hand. (Not that she'd left Michigan more than three times prior to Emma's birth, either.)

With the bag of peanut M&Ms in hand, Emma ripped through the top and wagged her eyebrows at her cousin, Megan, who sat on the other side of the aisle. Megan had lifted her head from a thick book written by Joyce Carol Oates.

"What's that, cuz?" Emma asked.

"I wanted to catch up on some reading before I head to State in August," Megan explained, closing the book on her thumb. "All the other students are going to be leaps and bounds ahead of me."

"That's impossible," Emma told her pointedly. "All you ever do at our apartment is read."

Megan rolled her eyes. "The makeup and dating magazines we've been reading over the past few years don't count."

"Why not?" Emma asked as Megan's lips twisted into a smile.

"You're going to visit, right?" It was probably the forty-fifth time Megan had asked her best friend and cousin this.

Emma flung her hands up, nearly toppling her Diet Coke. "Baby, I'll move in if you let me."

"It's a deal. We can share the bed like we used to." Megan giggled, then reopened her book, forcing her eyes back to the text.

Tracey sipped her wine, tracing the chilly liquid over her tongue. As the drink loosened her shoulders, she fell back against the seat and eyed her daughter, who now stared into the bag of peanut M&Ms as though it would reveal the secrets of the universe.

Tracey knew, in her heart of hearts, that Emma wasn't exactly thrilled that Megan planned to take this big step forward. Throughout their teenage years and now their twenties, they'd been thick as thieves, working side-by-side at the fudge shop, singing songs behind the counter, and eventually moving in together in the apartment up the stairs from the fudge shop itself. Neither had ever imagined that magical era to have an end.

But here it was. Megan was off to chase her dreams, majoring in Creative Writing at Michigan State University. Emma would be left at the fudge shop, wordless and song-less, reading through dating magazines alone. Tracey's heart ached for her. She remembered what it felt like to be aimless in her twenties before she'd founded the boutique. She wished she could point Emma down a road and say, "This one. Take this one." But selfishly, she knew that whatever road she opted for, she would make sure Emma stayed close to her if she could.

"You see a bug in there or something?" Tracey finally asked Emma.

Emma jumped, locking eyes with her mother. "Oh gosh. Sorry." She moved the bag of candy toward Tracey. "Have some. I forgot how good they are."

Tracey took several morsels into her hand. Not long afterward, the little pieces of candy began to melt their colors into her hand— orange, red, and yellow.

"Ugh. Gross." Tracey rubbed her napkin across her palm.

"That's why you have to eat them fast," Emma explained, getting her spunk back. She tossed one, two, then three more M&Ms into her mouth and chewed with a smile. "We're going to LA, Mama. It's fast-paced. No stragglers left behind."

"That's right!" Elise called proudly from behind them.

Tracey groaned. "Let's see if I survive this."

* * *

Within the first thirty minutes of Tracey's time in Los Angeles, the universe conspired against her.

Tracey, Elise, Penny, Megan, and Emma sat in the Baggage Claim area, chatting amicably and watching as various strangers walked past in every direction. Already, Tracey noted a marked difference between Californians and Michiganders— namely that Californians' outfits looked, on average, to be about two hundred dollars more expensive per person. Impressing strangers seemed to be the height of importance. Although Tracey adored fashion, she was grateful to live on Mackinac Island instead— a place where you could skinny-dip at the crack of dawn without a soul around (save for your bartender, that is).

There was no impressing anyone on Mackinac Island, anyway. Islanders knew you, through and through— had seen you embarrass yourself approximately four thousand times before the age of eight.

One after another, Penny, Elise, Megan, and Emma leaped up to grab their suitcases. Tracey eyed the black hole, where each suitcase popped out beneath a black flap.

Where was hers?

"It was pretty heavy," Emma teased. "Maybe it's at the very bottom of the plane. Maybe they needed at least ten strong men to heave it out."

"Funny girl." Tracey sniffed, her smile waning.

"I mean, there's no way that someone stole it without us seeing," Emma continued.

"Right, right. Because it's too heavy. I get it," Tracey returned, distracted.

Suitcases circled the baggage area around and around. Very soon, every single suitcase was claimed, and Tracey remained bagless, her heart pounding. Stricken, she turned to catch Elise's eye.

"I wanted to impress Donna so badly," she stuttered, sounding foolish. "I packed all those clothes thinking I could be..." *What? Another sort of person? The sort of woman ready to work in the wild world of film.*

Elise shook her head, a seasoned flier. "You don't know anything yet. Maybe your suitcase is somewhere else within the airport."

"How do I find that out?"

"Hmm. Ask someone?" Elise asked.

"Okay."

"Do you want me to come with you?" Elise's eyes were in slits.

"Don't worry about it. It's not a big deal." Tracey's brain sizzled with fear. Obviously, it was a very big deal. But she didn't want to sound like a drama queen or make it into something more than it should be. They'd arrived only thirty minutes before. *Everything else had to go smoothly.*

Tracey walked up to the nearest airport authority, a man in a bright yellow shirt and black tie who instructed her to fill out some paperwork in the next room. Tracey waved back to her crew, shrugging. Elise called out, "Remember, we're in no hurry." Tracey wasn't so sure.

Just before she walked through the automatic doors, Emma announced, "Mom! We're going to grab some coffee at the kiosk. Come find us there, okay?"

Tracey waved a hand, grateful that they wouldn't be

waiting around for her, eyeing the door with boredom. Since she was such an unpracticed flier, she couldn't help but blame herself for her idiocy. Perhaps she'd said something wrong to the airline worker back in Lansing, something that had led her to tag the bag with "**TO NEW YORK**."

The woman behind the counter looked dreadfully bored. She chewed her gum and clacked something out on the keyboard, which also looked like an antique. *Hadn't they updated their technology systems at Los Angeles International Airport?*

"Hi there." Tracey sounded even more nervous than she felt.

The woman kept typing for a full thirty seconds before she glanced up. Finally, she asked, "What can I help you with?"

Tracey explained the situation. It was simple enough, probably something the woman behind the counter heard over and over again. She barely reacted at all. In a flash, she smacked a clipboard on the counter and said, "You have your boarding pass? Flight number?"

Tracey nodded. She'd kept everything safe in her purse.

"Good. Fill out this paperwork. Come back to me."

Tracey eyed the tiny office, which was no bigger than a closet. A calendar hung on the wall and featured photographs of race cars. This couldn't have been more foreign to Tracey, who literally lived on an island without cars.

"Where should I go? To fill this out, I mean."

The woman gave her gum another four good chews before she pointed out the door. "There's some chairs in the lobby."

Tracey took a deep breath and stepped out into the hallway. Off to the right, she collapsed in a bright turquoise plastic chair and demanded herself not to cry. *Come on,* she told herself. *It's just a stupid piece of paper. Fill it out and be done with it.*

The first questions were easy. Name. Address. Date of

birth. Tracey breezed through them. Afterward, she hunted through her purse for her boarding pass, upon which she would find her flight number.

As she sat, stewardesses and pilots marched past, dragging wheeled suitcases behind them. Tracey paused her frantic search to eavesdrop on a group of three stewardesses, two of whom had British accents. Tracey shivered, wondering how many miles through the sky they'd flown in just that week. *How were they so fearless?*

Several of the pilots were just as good-looking as the movies told you. Others were a bit older, a bit rougher around the edges, but with this confidence in their stride, one that told you that they regularly had the lives of hundreds of people in their hands.

Tracey grew lost in watching the stewardesses and the pilots, eyeing their different uniforms— the yellows, purples, and oranges, the logos that told you which airline they worked for. She imagined an alternate reality in which she'd left the island at nineteen and become an airline stewardess, perhaps dating a pilot who flew her around the world.

Just when Tracey was about to convince herself to return her attention to her paperwork, a handsome, six-foot-two Delta Airlines pilot with dirty blonde hair and an arrogant jaunt marched down the hallway. He looked to be forty-eight, maybe forty-nine, with broad shoulders, a muscular torso, and long legs. His eyes were piercingly blue, the sort that made you stop in your tracks.

And for a long and terrifying moment, Tracey stared at him, completely shocked.

This man. This man before her.

Not only was he one of the most gorgeous people she'd ever met in her life. More than that, she knew him. Knew-him, knew-him. But she hadn't seen him in twenty-three years.

It was unquestionable.

For a long moment, the pilot and Tracey locked eyes. His stride didn't falter in the slightest. Tracey's lips parted in surprise. She remembered, with a strangely vibrant memory, the gorgeous way he'd used to kiss her— leaning her over backward on the beaches of Mackinac as the sun dropped into the Straits.

But just before she could call out his name, his eyes lifted from hers.

And, incredibly, he continued to walk down the hallway. He pressed open a door and disappeared from sight, leaving the door swinging closed behind him.

Tracey sat in stunned silence. She felt she'd been slapped hard across the face.

Like a zombie, Tracey filled out the rest of her paperwork and slid the clipboard across the counter. The woman with the gum told her that it would be processed "*as soon as possible*," whatever that meant. Then, she limped back down the hallway, her head swimming with fear.

Joey. Joey something. She'd never even known his last name.

"Mom. You good?" Emma's hands were wrapped around a thick cup of coffee. The eyes above it shimmered bright blue.

"Oh. Sure." Tracey could hardly hear herself.

"I guess they don't know where your bag is?" Elise pressed.

Tracey shook her head. Had all the blood gone to her feet? She teetered and fell into the nearest plastic chair.

"Mom?" Emma sounded stricken. "What's up?" She placed the cup of coffee on a nearby table and squatted next to her mother's chair.

"Oh, you know me. I just don't travel well," Tracey replied, blinking toward the far corner.

"We'll find you something to wear for tonight," Elise returned. "There are loads of boutiques and shops in Beverly Hills. It'll be fun."

Tracey nodded and forced herself to find her voice. "That sounds fantastic, Elise. Thank you."

Elise's smile was confused and fuzzy. Beside her, Emma glowered, sensing something deeper was amiss. But when Tracey offered up nothing else, Emma shrugged, leafed her arm through her mother's, and walked slowly out of the airport with her. As Emma listed the beaches that she and Megan planned to hit that week, Elise flailed an arm to hail a large cab, one that suited all five of them. Tracey slid into the chill of the vehicle's air conditioning, wondering if she was in some sort of version of hell.

Maybe she'd imagined it, though. Maybe it hadn't been Joey at all.

But she'd hardly thought about him in years. There was no way her mind could concoct that imaginary vision. Was there?

Chapter Four

Recently, Elise had sold her long-time house in Calabasas, setting aside the "old" to make space for her new life with Wayne, her fiancé on Mackinac Island. "It just means we have to rent something every time we're out here," Elise explained as the taxi drove to the side of the road in vibrant Beverly Hills. "Which isn't such a bad thing, right Pen? Means we can explore more of the city."

Tracey stepped onto the sidewalk, suitcase-less, her arms hanging limply at her sides. Above her, palm trees snaked into the sky and tossed easily through the breeze.

"This should be it." Elise pointed to a two-story home on the outer edge of Beverly Hills, a mini-mansion that had supposedly once belonged to Jennifer Love Hewitt. As they approached, the renter stepped out of the front door and greeted Elise, shaking her hand. Tracey was struck with how overtly tanned the woman was, as though she'd stood under tanning spray for five minutes too long. Was that the "popular look" in Los Angeles?

The renter gave them a tour, showing them the wine cellar

that kept the temperature at an exact seventy-two degrees, the dining room with a gorgeous view of the vegetable garden outside, the three bathrooms, one of which had a claw-footed tub, and the multiple bedrooms, enough for each woman to have her own. Although the Swartz family had grown up the richest family on Mackinac Island, the wealth before Tracey now seemed alien and out of this world. Her father, Dean, would take one look at it and laugh himself into a tizzy.

Tracey took the bedroom next to Emma's, across from Megan's. The bedroom featured a four-poster queen bed, an ornate mahogany desk, and a large, avant-garde painting of Elvis. Tracey sat at the edge of her bed, listening as Emma and Megan freaked out about their own rooms, the paintings and the ornate clocks and the thousand-count sheets on the bed.

"I never want to go back to the island again!" Emma exclaimed.

Tracey scrunched her nose, fearful at the truth behind Emma's words. She then dropped her body back and blinked at the ceiling, fearful. Why on earth had the universe put her and Joey in the same room again? It felt like a sign or a bad omen. She couldn't decide which.

* * *

1999

"Tell me, Tracey. Tell me. Who is it? Is it that Joey character you've been running around with?"

Tracey splayed a hand across her stomach. The pregnancy stick remained on the table between herself and her mother, Mandy: two bright pink lines which indicated that she'd "ruined her whole life."

"It's Joey, Mom." Tracey sniffed.

"And he's still here. He must be here. He's been here for months," Mandy blurted.

Tracey lifted her right shoulder to shrug. "He went out sailing last week."

"Okay. People go out sailing all the time, Trace."

"Yeah. But he never came back." Tracey took a staggered breath. "The guys at the docks say he isn't coming back."

Mandy smacked a fist across the table. Her eyes were blotchy and red with rage. "He left without saying goodbye. Honey, even if he didn't know you were..."

Tracey raised a hand between them. She didn't want her mother to insult Joey, the boy she'd raced around all summer long with hand-in-hand. He'd been her savior from a hazy summer of the same old people and the same old stories. She'd wanted to tell him she loved him, that she adored him. If she'd told him, would he have stayed? She would always wonder.

"It's for the best," Mandy stuttered. She began to pace up and down the long part of the table with her hands shoved in her apron pocket. "He wasn't going anywhere, anyway. Just another sailor, passing through." She then yanked herself around and stared down at Tracey, her eyes buggy. "I'll help you with this, honey. Every step of the way. You won't miss him, not for a day. From now on, he wasn't involved in this. Your child never had a father. Do you understand me?"

Tracey's throat tightened. She longed to tell her mother that she wanted to reach out to him, to tell him about the baby she now grew in her belly. But how on earth could she find him? He had no permanent address, no phone number. He was probably sailing across Lake Superior or the Atlantic Ocean by this point.

"This is for the best," Mandy continued. "Babies give you structure. They give you something to believe in." She sniffed. Tracey no longer knew if Mandy spoke about herself or about Dean or about just Tracey, her rather aimless daughter.

Finally, due to the severity of her mother's gaze, Tracey felt herself nod in agreement. "Okay, Mama," she whispered. "We'll raise the baby together. You and me and Cindy."

* * *

That night, Donna, the costume designer, several script supervisors, members of the fashion and creative team, and a few partners, husbands, and friends, greeted Tracey, Elise, Penny, Megan, and Emma at a Beverly Hills restaurant called Much Ado About Nothing. Tracey had to laugh at the name. People simply weren't as pretentious about stuff back on Mackinac Island. But what did she care? She had to play by California rules.

Emma sat beside Tracey, who'd glued a smile between her cheeks and dared herself to keep it going as long as possible. As the waiter brought over a large basket of bread, Emma leaned over to whisper, "You've been so weird since the airplane. What's wrong?"

Tracey shook her head and flashed her smile toward Donna, her new boss. Tracey, a business owner, hadn't had anything like a boss in decades, and the idea of someone to look up to thrilled her.

Donna was almost exactly what Tracey had imagined. She was tall, her shoulders bony, her elbows as sharp as bird talons. She wore a business suit jacket in bright white and wide-legged pants and spoke breezily about her yoga studio, a place, she said, that was "run by a sadist but gave you the firmest rear-end of your life."

Donna was also one of those people who liked to order for everyone else at the table. She pointed a manicured nail out to each and every member of the table, asking, "Tell me now or forever hold your peace. Are any of you vegetarian? Vegan?"

Penny raised her hand a half-inch before Elise smacked it

down. Donna pretended not to notice. Everyone else shook their heads.

"Good," Donna said. "I have quite a feast planned for us." Donna then instructed the server on the perfect array of cheese platters, chicken a l'orange, roasted green beans, pork cuts, various sorts of potatoes, and even some sausages, specially made in Germany. She also ordered wine for the table, which Tracey was grateful for. She didn't want to order something "incorrect" or "slightly cheap" in front of this gorgeous, worldly woman.

As they sipped wine and chatted, Elise said, "Tracey has done extensive research over the various time periods of Mackinac Island to ensure that each outfit in each scene is historically accurate."

Donna tilted her head with her wine lifted as she swirled the liquid around the inside of her palate before saying, "Is that so?"

Tracey felt put on the spot. "This story is very close to my heart. I want to do my part to ensure that every detail is precise."

"We'll have to compare notes later, Tracey."

Tracey's heartbeat quickened. She then turned her eyes toward Elise, awestruck. After a dramatic pause, Elise jumped in to pick up the slack.

"The screenplay joins our families together in a pretty beautiful and heart-wrenching way," Elise explained. "When I learned about Tracey's unique fashion talents, I knew she had to work alongside you."

Donna laughed good-naturedly. "And all this after the drama I've caused in my career?"

Elise pursed her lips. "Some say you're difficult to work with. I just say that they're..." She trailed off.

"I like 'weak,'" Donna finished.

Elise laughed. Tracey felt as though she'd just swallowed an ice cube; her throat and stomach grew chilly and strange.

"Say what you want," Elise encouraged her with the wave of her hand. "Donna is the best. And Tracey has enough innate talent and know-how to be in this world, absolutely. I believe the two of you will work well together."

Donna eyed Tracey curiously. Tracey had the sensation that Donna could see all the way through her. She swallowed, yearning to drop her gaze, but held it. She wanted to be viewed as a force of nature.

What had Joey seen her like, twenty-three years ago? Had he thought of her as a force of nature, one with the potential to keep him latched to Mackinac Island for good? Was that why he'd run away without saying goodbye?

Despite the trauma of the day, Tracey found herself falling into the splendor of the night— eating to her heart's content, listening to Donna's stories, and drinking the most delicious red wine of her life. Perhaps against her own wishes, Donna, herself, got tipsy, telling a few too many racy stories from her early days on set.

"I did have an affair with a quite famous director," she confessed, her voice low, almost sinister.

"Oh. Donna! Tell us everything," Emma cried.

Donna's eyes smoldered. "He was the most handsome and arrogant man I've ever dated in my life. Every time I saw him on set, I felt weak in the knees. I nearly fainted. I told my colleagues to keep a stretcher available every time he entered the room just in case I toppled over."

Everyone at the table cackled good-naturedly, grateful that Donna had allowed them to see a bit of her humanity.

Donna then dropped her chin, her eyes in slits. "Tell me there are some eligible bachelors on that island of yours."

Elise and Tracey locked eyes.

"Elise took one of the last ones," Tracey explained, smiling.

"Wayne told everyone he would never settle down again. Then, along came Elise to change his mind."

"Oh. That's right." Elise stretched her left hand out across the table. Her engagement ring glinted in the soft light.

"You're kidding. You're doing it again!" Donna shook her head.

Despite her forty-three years, Elise looked like a vibrant teenager on the brink of the rest of her life. "Sean and I had a very poisonous relationship. You remember that..."

Donna scrunched her nose. "Elise and I have known one another for decades. Decades! Since film school." She shook her head knowingly. "Sean was just as bright-eyed and optimistic as the rest of us. The only difference was, he wasn't any good at writing!"

Elise swatted Donna playfully, then gestured toward Penny. "You know this is my daughter, right? Penny?"

"Oh, honey. Are you his daughter? That means you know him better than me." Donna chuckled, then took another dramatic sip of wine.

Penny scrunched her nose. You could see it in her eyes: she agreed with Donna, yet she wasn't entirely sure she wanted to reveal it. Penny would always love her father, despite everything. Tracey understood this well. Although her father had cheated on her mother, her love for him allowed forgiveness. There was no other way.

"He's a really good accountant," Penny countered with a shrug.

To this, Donna tossed her head back, howling with laughter. "She's funny, Elise. Why didn't you tell me she was funny?"

"She's an actress," Elise replied with a dramatic sigh. "She can't help it. It runs in the family."

That night, cocooned with laughter and a nourishing kind of love, Tracey collapsed, fully clothed, in the four-poster bed from her deepest daydreams. As she shrugged herself out of the yellow dress she'd donned that moment, she dared herself to dream about the future— a world where Donna and Tracey ruled the costume department on set and created fictional worlds, all through the magic of beautiful vintage clothes.

Just before she drifted off to sleep, she half-remembered Joey, that scoundrel who'd marched back into her life and marched all the way back out. Perhaps she could think of it as "just another funny thing." Perhaps it wouldn't mean anything at all soon.

Chapter Five

Emma first understood the emptiness when she was maybe three or four. The questions came, as they so often do with toddlers. "Why don't I have a daddy like the other kids do?"

To Tracey's surprise, the questions always breezed past her. "Your daddy is out on an adventure right now, just like we are. Sometimes, daddies don't have the same adventures as mommies and children. But that's okay because we're just as strong and powerful and smart as all daddies— and we don't need them around. Do you understand?"

Perhaps because Emma and Tracey had always been thick as thieves, these questions had eventually filtered off. Emma knew not to touch the subject, not because it necessarily bothered Tracey, but because she sensed a black hole there. Nobody really knew where that vagabond Joey had ended up. Good riddance, Grandma Mandy had always said when Emma was out of earshot.

It was June 30th, just one day before their scheduled flight back to Michigan. After an outrageous work week, Tracey had allowed Emma and Megan to drag her to Santa Monica Beach, a daydreamy stretch of sand, where a Ferris wheel circled against a pink sky. Emma and Megan, now seasoned at the art of the California beach, stretched a large blanket across the sands, propped up a Bluetooth speaker, removed everything but their brand-new bikinis, and lay themselves down before the sun. Tracey, not twenty-two anymore, smeared suntan lotion across her arms, legs, stomach, neck, and face, remembering the wrinkles that peered back from the mirror. She made a comment about how the girls should "really take care of their skin," and both Emma and Megan grumbled and applied a light amount to their faces and shoulders.

When Tracey sat cross-legged beside her daughter, Emma lifted her sunglasses the slightest bit and said, "I can't believe we're heading home tomorrow already. I've totally fallen in love with California."

Tracey laughed, then gazed toward the thrashing waves. The Pacific was a wilder relative to their Straits of Mackinac, an entire ocean that stretched from North America to the impossible Asian continent.

"I'm ready," Tracey announced with a laugh. "The past week has been a doozy. Twelve-hour days of work, just poring over old vintage outfits and making notes about which outfits suit which scenes."

"Oomph. That's the kind of organization I need to learn for college," Megan joked.

"It's the kind of organization that would have made my life a whole lot easier before now," Tracey said.

"And how is it going with Donna?" Emma asked, shifting on the blanket.

"Oh." Tracey flared her nostrils. "She is a truly extraordinary woman. Overwhelming, yes. And perhaps..." She paused, searching for the right word.

Both Emma and Megan popped upright, ready for gossip.

Tracey laughed. "You're both girls after my own heart. Hungry for gossip, no matter what."

"Come on. What were you going to say?" Megan begged.

"She just seems a bit lonely," Tracey said, furrowing her brow. "She works these terribly long hours and has for decades. Elise was always just a screenwriter and able to make her own schedule. But if you're working on set, you're yanked from one area of the world to another. On the surface, it's glamorous. But for me..."

This time, Emma removed her sunglasses. "Is it too much? This job? Do you want to step away?"

Tracey thought her heart might burst. "No. I'll be mostly working on the island, bringing Elise's vision to life. How could I turn that down? Besides. You both will be on set several times as extras."

Emma and Megan exchanged glances, clearly worried and sensing something deeper beneath the surface of Tracey's initial fears. They were right. Tracey was terrified of so many things, areas of her mind and heart that she hadn't had to face throughout her entire career. Yes, Donna pushed her to the brink and demanded far more of her fashionable "intellect" than Tracey fully knew how to give.

But beyond that, she struggled to sleep, which made the twelve-hour workdays torturous.

Since she'd seen him at the airport, Joey had begun to appear in her dreams. This version was the twenty-something version, the one who'd said he "never wanted to keep down a steady job" because "steady jobs were for nerds and people without imagination." Tracey had thought all that to be really romantic back in the old days. Now, when Dream Joey spouted this "logic," she awoke sweating and panicked. It was like her psyche woke her up just to get her away from him.

Emma disappeared for a little while and returned with three corndogs, purchased from the Santa Monica docks.

Tracey laughed and said, "I don't think I've had a corndog in years."

"We've been addicted to them," Emma explained, dolloping a bit of mustard on the top of hers.

"Terrible for you," Megan said.

"Absolutely terrible," Emma echoed. "Which is why we adore them."

Tracey laughed, her stomach bouncing beneath the slick fabric of her one-piece suit. She took a small bite of cornbread and sizzling hot dog and closed her eyes. "It's immediate nostalgia, isn't it?"

Megan and Emma murmured their agreement.

Across the Pacific waves, surfers leaped upon their surfboards and whizzed over the waves, slicing back toward shore. Tracey took another bite of her corndog, listening as Emma and Megan discussed the shopping trip they planned to take to prepare for Megan's upcoming first semester of college. If Tracey wasn't totally amiss, she sensed that Emma pushed herself through the conversation, pretending to be just as excited for Megan as Megan was for her future. This, Tracey knew, was the sign of real love.

Back at their Beverly Hills mini-mansion, they found Elise and Penny in the kitchen over a collection of delivery menus. Shadows lurked beneath Elise's eyes, proof that she'd worked just as hard as Tracey had, just in a different sphere of the movie. Elise collapsed on top of Tracey mid-hug and laughed, saying, "Take me to bed. I can't even stay awake to eat."

But Penny waved a hand and replied, "Once you get Chinese food in front of her, she'll be just fine."

But the Swartz-Darby family didn't stop at Chinese. No. To celebrate their final night in Los Angeles, they ordered from each of Penny and Elise's favorite Beverly Hills restaurants, championing anything overly greasy and super sugary.

Together, they sat in the gorgeous living room, sipped wine, and waited for the immense amount of food they'd just ordered. A bit before it was officially "time," there was a crack at the door, and Penny opened it to discover Brad, her brother, who went to school at UCLA. Penny flung her arms around her brother, shrieking excitedly. Elise limped over and fell on top of her son, who laughed and said, "Ah, right. I forgot the way you get when you work on a movie."

"Brad, we have plenty of food coming," Penny explained, heading to the kitchen to fetch him a glass of wine and a stack of plates for their feast. "I hope you're staying?"

Brad lifted his arms up on either side of his muscular frame. "Hey. It isn't every day that your mother and sister are back in the city, huh?"

Penny burrowed her face in his shoulder, hiccupping with laughter. Tracey knew that normally, Penny attended college at Berkeley, outside of San Francisco. Since the end of last semester, she'd spent most of her time on the island, getting to know her mother's new fiancé, flirting with boys across the island, and pondering what she wanted to do "next" with her acting career.

Probably, she felt just as "in between and lost" as Emma and Megan did. This was just the nature of being twenty-something. Tracey couldn't speak for Brad. In fact, if she remembered Joey correctly, he'd seemed like a bright and confident light in the darkness, without a care in the world. Perhaps that same confidence had led him to become a pilot.

The food arrived. Tracey poured herself another hefty helping of wine and dug in— a bit of broccoli chicken, a couple of chicken tacos, a big serving of onion rings, and one-half of a cheeseburger. *Was it too much?* She laughed to herself, sipping another glass of wine. Emma, Megan, Penny, and Brad ate with sincerity, tearing through their food as they chatted. Only Elise and Tracey picked at their food, knowledgeable about metabolisms and what could happen if you gave it a chance.

God, how Tracey missed those long-ago days. Everything had been so carefree. Everything had simmered with magic.

* * *

It wasn't exactly a hard sell, getting herself to search for Joey online later that night. Her mind had raced through thoughts of him for nearly a week, making her borderline miserable. Heavy with food and buzzing with wine, Tracey lay on her stomach on the four-poster bed, listening to the twenty-somethings howl with laughter downstairs.

A problem, she knew, was that Joey had never given her his last name. Her mother, Mandy, had found this laughable. But as a very young woman, Tracey had found it romantic not to be "tethered to our families with our last names."

Still, she'd seen his uniform.

She knew enough to search.

JOEY - DELTA AIRLINES PILOT

She typed it and watched as her phone spit her forward to a result. **JOSEPH GILBERT.**

Joseph Gilbert. She whispered the name to herself a few times, trying it on for size. She read what she could about his piloting career— that he graduated from Arlington University and became a pilot at the age of thirty-two. That he was now based in Nashville, Tennessee, of all places. This meant that their spontaneous meeting had been just that much more spontaneous. What were the chances that he'd be in LA at the same exact moment she'd lost her luggage?

Tracey was surprised to see that Joey had a social media profile. This didn't align with the image of Joey she still had— a man who didn't need the outside world or its validation. She took a deep breath and clicked, imagining a vagabond man who took to the skies for comfort.

Instead, she found something much different.

Joey Gilbert was a family man.

Slack-jawed, she gaped at the first photograph that popped up. It was unmistakably Joey, a recent photograph. He stood in front of the Christmas tree, a toddler in his arms. A young girl, maybe six or seven, stood in front of him. A beautiful woman wore a genuine smile beside him: fresh lipstick, her eyebrows perfectly manicured, her smile bright as any Crest ad.

The woman in the photograph was tagged: Brittany Gilbert.

Suddenly, there was a rap at the door. In a flash, the door was open to reveal Emma and Megan, howling with laughter about something they wanted to explain to Tracey. Tracey felt herself lift up and heard herself answer them. She even heard herself laughing. *What had they said? What had she said? Did any of it matter?*

"What are you doing in here, Mom?" Emma asked as their laughter subsided.

"Oh. Nothing." Tracey forced a smile, one she knew Emma wouldn't believe. She blinked down at the phone on the bed, guilt filling her stomach. A thought rang through her mind. *Emma deserves to know. She always deserved to know everything.*

"You're acting weird," Emma shot out. "Come downstairs with us. Penny has a dating app installed, and we're making fun of everyone we see on there."

"A dating app?" Tracey giggled. "God, can you imagine if I used one of those things on the island? I'd run out of people to swipe in five seconds."

"It's a tiny place," Emma agreed. "But LA is enormous, with plenty of guys with absolutely atrocious tattoos. You have to see."

Tracey chuckled, swiping a fist across her eye. *Had she been crying? Why did she suddenly feel robbed of a life she should have had?*

"All right. All right. I'll come see," Tracey said, dropping her feet onto the lush rug beneath the bed.

Megan gave her a curious smile. "Okay. We've made a game out of it. Every time we see a guy with a snake tattoo, we take a drink. Every time we see a guy with a face tattoo, we take a shot. And every—"

"I think I get the gist," Tracey said, chuckling.

As she padded down the stairs after her daughter and niece, she felt the weight of what she'd just learned. It felt like an animal digging through the caverns of her mind. How could she move on, knowing that Joey had built a whole family with a woman named Brittany and become an airplane pilot on top of it all?

Should she have fought harder to find him?

Should she have fought harder to build the family life she and Emma had deserved?

Chapter Six

It was incredible timing, really. The following morning, in the taxi on the way to the airport, the airline contacted Tracey to say that they'd just shipped her suitcase back to Michigan.

We hope that you'll fly with us again, the airline said in the email. Tracey scoffed and showed the email to her daughter, who chuckled, pressing her hand against her mouth. She turned green soon after, proof she was probably hungover and slightly carsick as a result. Tracey prayed they would make it to LAX in peace.

The vehicle line outside the airport was long and staggered them forward bit-by-bit. Tracey wasn't worried. Elise had requested that they arrive at the airport two and a half hours early, already worried about issues like this.

"We don't want to walk a half-mile with our suitcases," Elise affirmed from the front seat of the cab, her eyes still pointed toward her phone. "We have time."

Emma closed her eyes and leaned her head on Tracey's shoulder. In the very back seat, Megan and Penny both texted with quicker fingers than Tracey had ever managed. Tracey smoothed her daughter's hair and tried to wrap her mind around yet another plane trip. It seemed insane to her that anyone ever got used to it.

Her phone buzzed. Yet again, she had more messages from Donna, who seemed like an anxious wreck so soon before the official start date of the shoot.

DONNA: I'm having trouble locating those old-fashioned umbrellas we talked about. Do you remember where we put them in the warehouse?

Tracey pressed her lips together, trying to visualize where they'd arranged the seventies-style umbrellas, perfect for two scenes in the upcoming film. Her thumbs roamed the screen, trying to come up with an answer.

But before she could scribe an answer back, her phone buzzed between her palms. Annoyed, thinking it was just Donna saying, "Sorry, I found them!" Tracey dropped her gaze to the phone, her nostrils flared.

But instead, a notification told her something far different. It was from her social media account, and it said:

JOEY GILBERT wants to send you a message.

Tracey's heartbeat pounded from ear to ear. For about thirty seconds, she forgot how to breathe. She continued to blink at that notification, wondering if, somehow, she'd fallen asleep in the taxi and dreamed this up because there was no way. *Right? No way.*

But there was only one way to find out.

Tracey's tentative thumb clicked on the notification.

And suddenly, there they were— the seven words that made her yearn to change her life forever.

JOEY: Did I see you at the airport?

* * *

"I would love a glass of wine. Please." Tracey blinked wide-eyed at the airline stewardess. Beneath her, the plane bumped over a patch of air. Several people on the plane gasped, fearful. But Tracey was no longer frightened of turbulence, not really. There was a whole lot more to worry about.

"I'll just have a Diet Coke," Emma said, giving the stewardess a sheepish smile.

"Anything to eat?" Tracey asked.

Emma shook her head sadly, accepting the bubbling drink.

"We'll rest up when we get home," Tracey told her daughter— and herself. "It's a long weekend. We have plenty of time to sleep, hang at the beach, eat delicious food, and celebrate Fourth of July."

"Thank goodness," Emma breathed.

Emma eventually fell asleep, her head knocking about on Tracey's shoulder. Throughout the flight, Tracey dared herself to look at the message on her phone, an impossible sentence that seemed to exist in another world. *Did she dare write back? And what on earth would she say?*

Maybe she could respond: *Yes. What a coincidence!*

That would stop the conversation in its tracks, acknowledge the weirdness of life, and send them both on their separate paths.

But did she actually want that?

What if she said: *You're a pilot with a beautiful family. How wonderful.*

Or: *Why wasn't I enough for you?*

Or:

Well. There really wasn't a right way, was there? Their paths had crossed again. And with this message, Joey basically confessed that his mind had been burning with curiosity about her since then, just as hers had.

She could write: *You're married. We can't.*

But how presumptuous was that? It wasn't like he'd written

anything overly romantic or fantastical. It was just a question sent out into the universe. She didn't have to write back at all.

* * *

It seemed easier to ignore the message. Back at the Lansing Airport, Tracey shoved her phone deep in her purse and followed after Emma and Elise, rolling the brand-new, much smaller suitcase behind her in which she'd packed her California wardrobe. Outside, Michigan humidity steamed them, frizzing up their hair. Emma laughed and wagged her head like a dog, frothing her hair around.

"I miss California," she said.

"I miss California guys," Megan quipped.

"No, I promise you. You don't," Penny said, elbowing Megan. "I've had more than my share of heartache. California guys are obsessed with themselves."

"And Michigan guys?" Emma asked.

"They're so sweet!" Penny bit her lower lip, as though she had a secret.

Megan and Emma exchanged knowing glances. Tracey and Elise shared one, as well.

"All right. Everyone in the car," Elise ordered, popping the trunk of the SUV rental she'd driven them down in.

One after another, they slid their suitcases into the back trunk and buckled themselves into the car— Penny up front, and Tracey, Emma, and Megan in the back. As they drove back up to Mackinac Island, they bounced from radio station to radio station, singing classic hits from the nineties and two-thousands and chatting about the tremendous week they'd had in California.

The sixteen-minute ferry ride from Mackinaw City to Mackinac Island left Tracey speechless. Throughout, she stood on the top deck, her hands around the iron railing as she watched her gorgeous tree-covered island grow bigger and bigger on the horizon line. Across the western sky, the sunset became a staggering smear of maroons and purples and blues. Captivated, Tracey dropped her lips to whisper into Emma's ear, "Can you believe we get to call this place our home?"

Emma grimaced and didn't say anything. Tracey's heart dropped into her stomach. She considered apologizing for being too "cheesy" but bit hard on her tongue to stop herself. There was no telling what lurked in that twenty-two-year-old's head.

Later that evening, Tracey sat on her back porch with a glass of lemonade, watching the black night crawl across the sunset-filled sky. Her suitcase remained on her bed, unpacked, and her phone was filled with another ten messages from Donna, asking more clerical questions about the upcoming shoot. Tracey had all but begged Emma to come home with her, to sit wordlessly on the back porch with her and watch the day fade away. But Emma had admitted to being "zonked." "I have a shift tomorrow morning. I need to pull myself together," she'd said.

As though she sensed the unrest in Tracey's soul, Cindy called. Tracey answered it hungrily. She so needed to hear the sound of a loved one's voice.

"You're back!" Cindy called.

"I am."

"You must be exhausted."

Tracey laughed quietly. "I don't know if I've ever been this tired." *Tell Cindy what happened. Tell Cindy about Pilot Joey. You have to get these things off your chest.*

But instead, Tracey asked, "What have you been up to?" It was always better to deflect.

"Goodness. Well. Ron came over for dinner tonight," Cindy began.

"Oh. Ron!" Tracey's grin widened. "Things are really heating up between you two."

Cindy groaned. "I don't know why I tell you anything. You're shameless."

Tracey's stomach flipped over with happiness. If there was anything she wanted to believe in, it was her sister's joy, especially in the wake of her ex-husband's volatility and emotional abuse. Fred had recently left the island, allowing Cindy, Michael, and Megan a new lease on life— to write a story that had nothing to do with him. Cindy's budding romance with Ron was a part of that.

"And you? I want to hear every detail of your time in California," Cindy said.

Tracey's heart seized. This was her chance. Her phone burned with Joey's message, an attempt to drag her back into the depths of her long-dormant emotions.

"I don't think I've ever worked harder in my life," Tracey said instead. "My boss, Donna, is a real piece of work."

"You haven't had a boss in decades," Cindy pointed out. "The curse and benefit of being your own boss for so long."

"Thanks for saying that." Tracey dropped her chin to her chest. There was a moment of silence. Cindy clearly waited for Tracey to continue, to describe the food on the west coast or the rudeness of Californians. But Tracey's exhaustion made her limp. Soon, Cindy chatted easily about all things Ron, about her fear that Marcy had spread gossip about their early-morning skinny-dipping, about Michael's pregnant girlfriend, and about Megan's approaching move to Michigan State University. Tracey was grateful to fall into the warmth of Cindy's words. She wowed and laughed her way through the conversation until her yawns were so powerful that Cindy told her to "crawl into bed this instant." She did as she was told and slept a dreamless sleep.

* * *

The weekend was a flurry of activity. Temperatures rocketed to the mid-eighties, and tourists flocked across the island, biking along the coastline, hiking the woods, and eating at the gorgeous restaurants along the waterline. Tracey kept her distance from crowds, cleaning her house, enjoying early-morning runs with Cindy, and finally welcoming the return of her massive suitcase from the airline, which was banged up on the outside but wholly intact within. All the while, she avoided her social media like the plague. Joey's message was like a bomb waiting to go off.

On the afternoon of the Fourth of July, Emma and Megan ambled up the front stoop, catching Tracey in the midst of an intense work session. Donna and Tracey had decided to restructure some of the lists and spreadsheets for the upcoming shoots, a task that Tracey had volunteered to take over since Donna was still on the frontlines of having all the costumes delivered from LA to Mackinac.

"What? Working on the Fourth?" Emma teased, kissing her mother's cheek. "That isn't like you."

Tracey waved a hand, removing her reading glasses. "Donna's intensity reaches all the way across the continent. But she's right. We don't have long before the first day of shooting. I want everything to be perfect before the cameras roll that first day."

Megan nodded solemnly. "You've thrown yourself into this. It's amazing to see."

"It is! I'm not saying it isn't. I'm just saying, it's the Fourth of July, and as Swartz women, it's our mission to eat hot dogs, potato salad, watermelon, and s'mores to our heart's content," Emma countered.

"Right. Nothing says, 'God Bless America' like a big helping of potato salad," Megan affirmed. "Plus, Mom says if we're not up at the house by two, we'll miss most of the festivities."

Tracey chuckled, imagining Cindy's current state: running around the house like a chicken with her head cut off. Every year, she held the Swartz Family Fourth of July Barbecue—arranging grocery purchases, serving buckets of alcohol, putting Fred in charge of the grill, and forcing a level of "family fun" that lasted until the final fireworks burst over the Straits of Mackinac.

This year would be the same, save for Fred— with the addition of Michael's girlfriend and, of course, Elise and Penny. The change was inevitable, Tracey knew. She was glad they were able to welcome it.

Tracey sent a final email to Donna, sliced a watermelon, gathered three bottles of wine in a tote bag, and buttoned a navy-blue dress from her thighs to the top of her chest. Emma and Megan chatted in the kitchen, waiting for her. Mostly, the conversation circled a bit of drama at the fudge shop, where Megan had suddenly grown resistant, annoyed at yet another summer of angry tourists and their boss's inability to experience empathy. "God, I can't wait to get out of here," Megan said.

To this, Emma said, "I don't blame you."

Tracey's stomach twisted with worry. She hustled toward the kitchen, tearing through their conversation as she said, "You two ready to go?" They gathered the tote bag, the sliced watermelon, the bags of fudge the girls had taken from the shop, and packages of graham crackers, chocolate, and marshmallow, which they would soon merge together to form gooey s'mores.

All Tracey could pray for was a distraction from her aimless thoughts and worries. All she could hope for was a gorgeous afternoon spent with the people she loved most.

Chapter Seven

Tracey's imagined picture of Cindy "running around like a headless chicken" couldn't have been more incorrect. The Cindy who opened the door of the old Victorian House on the hill was shamelessly thrilled to see them, with bright red lipstick and a dress to match, her hair curled and her perfume wafting about her like a cloud. She hugged her daughter first as she chirped out her greeting.

"Go out back! Dad's already doing his best to ignore the vegetable platter I set out on the table and focus on the chips and cheese instead." Cindy accepted Tracey's tote bag and hugged her next, squeezing her tightly as she whispered, "And Ron should be over within the hour, too."

Tracey followed Emma and Megan to the back porch, where her father, Dean Swartz, sat in a blue button-down. His Labrador, Diesel, panted at his feet, his mouth curling upward into a sort of smile. True to form, Dean had a chip lifted as he nodded along to whatever Wayne said. As they were both widowers, the two of them had developed an unlikely yet welcomed friendship over the years, which had strengthened all the more when Wayne had fallen in love with Dean's "surprise" child, Elise.

Elise herself stood behind Wayne, her beautiful hands across his shoulders. Elise brightened at the sight of Tracey.

"Oh good. I thought I'd die by way of sports-talk torture," Elise said.

"Lucky for you, I don't know a thing about sports," Tracey affirmed. She lifted a patio chair from the corner and sidled up alongside Elise, who poured Tracey a glass of wine without asking. Tracey thanked her and clinked the glass to hers. In the opposite corner, Megan and Emma sat with Michael and Margot, whose stomach bulged cartoonishly toward the sky. Tracey waved good-naturedly, and the young couple waved back, grinning overzealously, as though, with their pregnancy, they'd discovered the secret to eternal happiness. Boy, they were in for a rough ride.

When Ron arrived, Cindy set him up at the grill, a place he seemed content to remain. Tracey didn't blame him. Dating someone for the first time after his wife's passing was probably not easy; dealing with that woman's family was a whole other beast. That said, Tracey did her best to include him in the conversation, asking him about how he felt the Lilac Festival had gone that year and how he felt about an entire year on Mackinac Island without retreating south for the winter. Ron took each question graciously.

Just before the burgers finished sizzling on the grill, Tracey's younger brother, Alex, stepped onto the porch. As per usual, he looked slightly paler than summer should have allowed, as though he still spent most gorgeous days latched behind a desk. Alex took his position as "manager" of Dean's properties incredibly seriously, usually to a fault. Tracey often asked herself if Alex would ever push himself to find the kind of happiness he deserved.

She could ask herself the same sort of question, she supposed.

As the Swartz family licked their plates clean and settled into the afternoon, Elise clacked her fork against the side of her wine glass. "Everyone. We have an announcement." Her grin was enormous, showing nearly all of her California white teeth.

"That's right." Wayne lifted Elise's hand and pressed his lips onto it. "We've set the date for the wedding."

Elise brimmed with joy. "October 22nd. I've always dreamed of an autumn wedding. All those incredible colors and the crisp air..."

"Congratulations!" Cindy cried, wrapping her arms around Ron, swimming in her own endless happiness.

"This is incredible news," Dean affirmed. "Wow." He stood on creaking legs and extended his arms on either side of him. Wayne stepped into the hug, followed by Elise.

The back porch exploded with life and conversation. Everyone had something to say about this newly decided wedding date and the change it would bring. Only Tracey felt soft and unsure, watching the manifestations of a beautiful couple who'd dared to dream for something beyond their own misery.

Eventually, noticing how quiet Tracey remained, Elise hustled over to Tracey to thank her again for helping her pick out her wedding dress.

Tracey, laughing, poured herself another glass of wine. *Was this her third? Maybe her fourth?* She couldn't remember. "I can't wait to figure out what to wear. It's not every day your newly discovered half-sister marries a dear friend you've known for decades."

"That is very specific." Elise chuckled.

In the distance, a firework exploded spontaneously. The sound crept across the island, proof that very soon, the Straits of

Mackinac would be filled with colorful fire. It was still a little too early, a couple of hours before the air would be heavy with darkness, the perfect backdrop.

"I think it's time for a s'more," Emma insisted, grabbing several marshmallows from the plastic bag, and adding them to the far end of an iron stick.

"Oh, same." Margot waddled toward the sticks. Michael hustled over to help her, shooing her back to her seat.

"I haven't seen you move that quickly in a while," Michael teased.

Margot laughed, her hands pressed hard against her lower back for support. "I'll do anything for a s'more."

"S'more of what?" Dean asked, his smile mischievous. This was a longstanding joke. One Dean had stolen from the movie, *The Sandlot.*

"You know, Grandpa. S'mores..." Michael said, rolling his eyes.

"I get it. I get it. But s'more of what?" Dean asked.

"You're just like a child," Cindy said, waving a hand.

Alex, who'd hardly spoken throughout the dinner party, took several quick steps toward the marshmallow bag and soon lifted his own marshmallow over the coals. "You remember how much Mom loved that movie?"

Tracey's heart was squeezed a little at the memory. "I remember. She made us watch it with her on rainy days in the summertime."

"Your mother was one of the most nostalgic people I ever knew," Dean replied. "It was almost like her superpower. She could find emotion in anything."

Alex's eyes swam with tears. Tracey watched as he hurriedly blinked them away. He then stepped back toward the table and pressed the melted marshmallow onto one-half of a graham cracker and squares of chocolate before squishing the marshmallow with another square of graham cracker.

"Now, that's a man who knows his way around a s'more," Wayne pointed out.

Alex laughed for perhaps the first time that day and passed the s'more over to his father. Dean lifted his hands to wave it away.

"I couldn't. It's too perfect. You should eat it," Dean told his son.

But Alex shook his head. "I made it for you, Dad."

Dean's eyes softened. He accepted the gift and crunched at the edge, his eyes closing. After he'd swallowed his first bite, he said, "Melted chocolate. Gooey marshmallow. Perfect ratio. My boy, you've done it again."

"Come on, Michael. My food envy is insane right now!" Margot called.

"Nobody does s'mores like the Swartz Family," Cindy said matter-of-factly. "Everyone knows that."

Ron's eyes glittered knowingly. "I guess you'll have to teach me your ways."

Tracey blinked away tears that she couldn't quite explain. What was it she felt? Joy? Sorrow? Jealousy? She sipped her glass of wine, conscious that she hadn't had anything to say in quite some time. In the corner, Emma and Megan whispered conspiratorially. Megan laughed at something Emma said, her eyes clenching.

With a strange jolt, she wondered: *Would Joey have liked this life? Would he have made s'mores and laughed with Dean? Would he have teased Emma and kissed Tracey's hand in front of the rest of the family?*

Did he have this kind of life with his "real" family?

A little while later, Tracey stood, her legs heavy and quivering beneath her. Cindy locked eyes with her across the table, her smile wavering. Tracey gave her a confident smile and headed for the back door, slipping into the cool shadows of the large house. Once alone, in the silence, she leaned against a white wall and slid down toward the ground. She sat like a ball with her arms wrapped around her legs.

And before she knew what she'd done, her thumbs typed furiously over her phone screen— texting an answer to Joey's reckless question.

JOEY: Did I see you at the airport?

TRACEY: Yes. I saw you, too. But it was like seeing a ghost.

Tracey sent the message off and gaped at it, terrified of the response she would get. What had she done? She shoved the phone deep into her pocket and gulped her wine.

No more than three minutes later, her phone pinged with a message from Joey, her ghost.

JOEY: I haven't been able to stop thinking about you since I saw you.

JOEY: Are you still on Mackinac Island?

Tracey blinked at the black words on her screen. It was a surprise that Joey Gilbert even remembered where in the world they'd met. Based on what she knew about his previous antics, Joey probably had at least ten Tracey's (and maybe a handful of Emma's) across the continent.

Tracey told herself to throw her phone across the room. She told herself not to continue opening this can of worms.

But instead, she watched herself write back.

TRACEY: I am. I never could imagine myself anywhere else.

Joey wrote back in a split-second, proof that he cradled his phone, waiting for her response.

JOEY: I couldn't imagine you anywhere else, either. And why would you leave? It's paradise up there.

JOEY: I'm in Nashville now. Based there, anyway.

TRACEY: And you're a pilot?

JOEY: Surprised that I got my life together?

Tracey bubbled with laughter.

TRACEY: Not exactly. I suppose we all get there, one way or another.

JOEY: Did you find a way to grow up?

Tracey's thoughts burned with a thousand different images, most of which involved Emma and the duties required of Tracey as a single mother.

TRACEY: I go days thinking I'm still a teenager. I guess that's the thing about getting older. You can trick yourself into thinking it didn't happen at all.

"Mom?" Emma stepped out from behind the screen door. Her eyes dropped to Tracey, wrapped tightly in a ball on the floor. "What are you doing?"

Tracey's cheeks burned with embarrassment. She hurried to her feet, dropping her phone back into her pocket. On cue, it buzzed with a message back from Joey.

"Nothing. Just fielding messages from Donna," Tracey lied.

"Can't that woman take a day off?" Emma asked.

Tracey lifted a shoulder sadly.

"Come on. The fireworks should be starting soon. We're going to sit on the front porch," Emma explained.

Cindy's back porch wrapped around to the front, where the Swartz family enjoyed a picture-perfect view of the Straits of Mackinac and the Mackinac Bridge. Tracey sat wordlessly as her family chattered around her, nibbling snacks, drinking wine, and celebrating their country's birth.

When she thought she could get away with it, Tracey grabbed her phone and read Joey's recent messages.

JOEY: You were always so insightful. More

worldly than your little island should have allowed.

JOEY: Tell me. What's your life like these days?

Tracey blinked back tears. It was so nourishing to think that the man she'd had a child with actually still cared about her in some abstract way.

"What are you doing over there?" Cindy asked suddenly, yanking Tracey from her reverie.

"She's texting Donna," Emma explained, crunching on a chip.

"Yeah. It's just Donna," Tracey said with a shrug.

"Come on, Tracey. Donna should understand that you have family responsibilities," Elise countered. "If she doesn't, she had better learn."

Tracey placed her phone in her purse and grabbed a chip, forcing herself back into the family discussion. All the while, Cindy eyed Tracey curiously, as though she sensed something amiss.

As the first firework explosions burst over the Straits, Cindy dropped her chin to whisper, "Are you sure you're okay?"

Tracey locked eyes with her sister. For years, Tracey had upheld telling the truth above all things. But what good would talking about this Joey situation do for any of them?

"Oh. Yeah." Tracey shrugged at Cindy crossing her arms.

Cindy's whisper came, raspy and uneven. "Is it a guy?"

Tracey rolled her eyes into the back of her head. In truth, Tracey had been something of a serial dater over the years. Normally, she'd hidden her small-time relationships from Emma, wanting to uphold a sense of normality. Besides, it wasn't like the guys stuck around for long.

"It's not such a crazy thing to ask," Cindy said, clearly hurt by Tracey's eye roll. "It's been a little while since..."

Tracey waved a hand. "I don't need my sister to remind me how long it's been since I had a date."

Cindy grimaced, dropping her eyes. "I didn't mean it that way."

Tracey dropped her head against the back of the patio chair. Each firework explosion sent vibrations up her arms and legs. Deep in her phone, Joey's messages rang through, buzzing all throughout the night. Tracey felt on the brink of a new era of life, one that terrified her.

But if there was anything she believed in, it was second chances. Maybe it was finally time for hers.

Chapter Eight

"This humidity! Tracey, why didn't you warn me?" Donna stepped out of one of the costume trailers, ruffling her fingers through her hair. She wore a linen pantsuit, and her hair had recently been trimmed around her ears, which made her hair poof up clownishly.

Tracey had several pins in her lips. She was hard at work, altering an outfit for one of the extras in the very first scene they planned to shoot on Mackinac Island. All she could do was grunt in return.

Around them, a flurry of activity spread out across the waterline and grounds in front of The Grand Hotel. According to Donna, the studio could only get the rights to film on the grounds of the famous hotel during the week of July 11, which made everything furiously important, stressful, and unorganized.

Tracey was in charge of upwards of fifteen extras, most of whom were islanders she'd known her entire life. Nervous about being in a film at all, they were silent and big-eyed, paying attention to Tracey's every demand. Tracey stuck a pin into the top of an older woman's dress, adjusting it so that it hung higher up on the chest.

"There you go, Brenda."

"Thanks." Brenda looked sheepish. "I was a bit worried to reveal so much of myself on camera!"

Tracey laughed good-naturedly, assessing the rest of her extras. She then turned on a heel and led them out across the grounds of The Grand Hotel, where the assistant director informed each of them where to stand. Tracey bubbled with anticipation and alternated between wanting to sob and wanting to laugh.

When Tracey returned to the sidelines, Donna bent down to whisper, "They look good, Tracey. Really good. Now, just watch them during the shot. See if their outfits change or hang incorrectly afterward. You'll need to run in and out of the shot between takes to fix everything."

Tracey nodded, her eyes filling with tears. Donna began to discuss the intricacies of the main actor and actress in the current scene, what they wore, how they wore it, and whether it actually worked in the shot.

"Think it might be too late to change anything, though," Donna explained, disgruntled. "See the director over there?"

Tracey's eyes dropped to the stoic-looking man seated in the director's chair. He wore a black baseball cap without a logo, a black t-shirt, and a pair of black jeans. He looked exceedingly LA.

"His name is Malcolm Ritter," Donna explained. "He was a hotshot, up-and-coming director several years back. He disappeared for a while. Nobody knew why. Now, he wants to use this project to become a rising star director again."

"It's good he's passionate about it, right?" Tracey asked.

Donna groaned. "I don't know. In my experience, if someone's ego is tied up too much in a project, there are a lot of casualties."

"Casualties?" Tracey asked.

"Quiet on the set!" an assistant director wailed, slashing his arms through the air.

Tracey snapped her lips shut, becoming hyper-focused on the costumes of the extras and whether or not they shifted at all during the shoot. She and Donna peered down at a screen that showed them precisely what the shot looked like.

Only once Tracey allowed herself to think: Wow. I'm really doing it. I'm a part of movie magic.

The take wasn't a long one. In it, the main actor and actress discussed what it meant to fall in love, especially if that love couldn't last forever. Around them, extras walked around the grounds of The Grand Hotel, enjoying their fictional vacations.

When the scene finished and the director cried, "Cut!" Tracey hustled back into the shot to fix outfits and adjust necklines and position the extras back in their original places. There was no telling how many times the director would want to capture that same scene. As she continued to pin clothes and clean shoes of grass stains, Malcolm Ritter, the director, spoke to the main actor and actress about the way they'd said their lines. "I need you to pause more between these lines," he explained to the actress. "The viewer needs to feel your hesitance."

Tracey caught herself listening to the director a little too earnestly. He sounded terribly stoic and intense. She lifted her eyes to catch the outline of his face, the dark fuzz of his eyebrows, and the sharp line of his jaw. *Why had he disappeared from the movie world for so long? What had happened to him? Had he burned himself out?*

"Quiet on the set!" the assistant director howled again.

Tracey leaped from the shot and hustled over to where

Donna stood, already staring into the screen. Already, Tracey sensed just how long this day would go. It was only nine in the morning, and Donna had told her multiple times that the majority of their shoots continued until eight or nine at night.

Unfortunately for the film crew, however, this was Michigan, not California.

And just after lunchtime, sinister clouds circled overhead, thickening and casting everyone in their shadow.

"It isn't supposed to rain!" the assistant director wailed. "I checked the weather numerous times. This is ridiculous."

The actor and actress eyed one another fearfully, as though the rain was made of acid. Donna grumbled, "I wonder how many more shots we can squeeze in before the rain comes."

Malcolm Ritter was a man with a mission. He howled to everyone, "Calm down. We're going to get as many shots as we can until this surprise storm comes. If we get behind on day one, there's no telling where we'll be a month from now. Now, go-go-go, people! Set back up!"

When the actor and actress returned to their original stances far down The Grand Hotel grounds, however, Tracey noted that the actress's dress hung crooked. Donna was tending to something off to the side, scribbling a note to herself. Tracey was faced with a moral dilemma. *Should she bother Donna with this very small detail? Or should she just fix it herself?*

Being a Swartz woman, she knew the answer already.

Tracey rushed out across the lush grass, greeting the actress warmly. With urgent motions, she lifted the seventies-style skirt and pulled it off to the right.

"Goodness. I didn't even notice how wrong that was!" The actress thanked her warmly.

"Did someone not hear me? I need to get as many shots as possible before the storm comes!" Malcolm Ritter barked across the grounds. "Can the costuming department get their act together? Jesus. Don't they get how important this is? Don't they get that we can't dillydally?"

Tracey's face crumpled. She turned on a heel and hustled back from the shot, her shoulders shaking. Over and over again, Tracey told herself not to cry, that it wasn't worth it.

When Tracey reached the sidelines again, Donna glowered. Tracey pointed back toward the actress, wanting to explain. But instead of allowing it, Donna said, "You need to develop much thicker skin, Tracey. Otherwise, there's no way you'll survive this shoot."

Tracey's lips parted with surprise. She'd expected Donna to be on her side. In fact, she'd expected Donna to tell her how proud she was that Tracey had noticed the skirt issue in the first place.

That was naive. Tracey saw that now.

"When he gets like that, you have to listen to everything he says," Donna continued under her breath. "He's like a bomb about to go off at any time."

Tracey sloped her shoulders forward, watching the scene play out for the tenth time. This time seemed almost perfect. Tracey would have been gobsmacked to learn that it wasn't good enough. Just as the scene finished, a clap of thunder rattled across the sky. Malcolm Ritter cursed loud enough for most of the staff members to hear.

"All right. Pack up, everyone. We got the shot."

Tracey flung into action, draping plastic over the extra's outfits, and fitting large racks of clothing onto the trailers. Just as the last of the equipment was packed away, fat raindrops splattered her arms, legs, and cheeks.

Donna ruffled her fingers through her damp hair. She gave Tracey a firm nod and said, "Remember. Thick skin. Otherwise, we won't make it longer than a few days together."

Tracey's stomach twisted. *Was that a threat?*

"Got it," Tracey told her.

"I hope so." Donna coughed, then eyed the black clouds above her. "There was a reason I moved to LA. I'd forgotten." She then ducked into the rain, lifting an umbrella above her.

Soon afterward, Tracey walked home in the rain, shivering, her clothing drenched. A part of her ached with missing her little boutique, which she'd decided to only open on her "off" days from the film shoot. There, she was her own boss, communing with customers and playing her own music. No volatile directors screamed at her; no wicked costume designers told her to "thicken her skin."

Drenched, Tracey sat in the solitude of her front porch and grabbed her phone. Since their Fourth of July correspondence, Tracey and Joey had kept up a consistent back-and-forth—usually just bantering about the past.

This time, Tracey longed for an affirmation from an old friend. She longed for comfort.

TRACEY: I started working in the costume department of a film here on the island today.

TRACEY: It was difficult. Intense. Like my skills weren't enough.

Tracey puffed out her cheeks. She could practically feel the message rushing out across Michigan, Indiana, Kentucky, and, finally, Tennessee. It marked time and distance between Tracey and Joey, two star-crossed lovers. At least, that's what she'd begun to tell herself.

It was irresponsible. She knew that.

JOEY: Wow! Costuming for film?

JOEY: You were always the most fashionable woman I knew.

JOEY: I can't imagine that you're not killing it. It's probably just a fast-paced, intense environment. You can't take everything on set personally.

I'm sure whatever happened, everyone has already forgotten about it.

Tracey's heart lifted. She pressed the phone against her chest, dropped her head against the back of the chair, and listened to the steady pat-pat of the rain. Oh, if only Joey was there, his strong arms around her. If only he could whisper these truths to her in person. If only.

Chapter Nine

The next few days passed in a flurry of anxiety-heavy hours on set. Miraculously, the Michigan rains subsided and allowed the film crew countless sun-filled takes in front of The Grand Hotel. These were scenes that captured the way The Grand Hotel had been back in the seventies, along with scenes that captured a more modern-day Grand. Tracey kept her head down and worked herself like a dog, grateful, now, that when Malcolm Ritter decided to lash out at someone, it usually wasn't her. Usually.

That Friday afternoon, Tracey collapsed at the lunch table over a chicken burrito and placed her face in her hands, exhausted. Donna sat across from her, chewing at the edge of a quesadilla as she scribbled notes to herself. Tracey couldn't remember the last time she'd seen the woman take a second to herself. She couldn't remember her even taking a moment to run to the bathroom.

Donna lifted her pen to her lips and chewed at the edge. Tracey saw this as an opening.

"Have you had any chance to enjoy the island since you got here?"

Donna looked at Tracey as though she'd just spoken Chinese. "I can't imagine doing anything but sleeping and returning to set," she said, laughter bubbling through her. "Gosh, to have the time to explore the island! That would be a dream."

Tracey's cheeks burned. It had been a stupid question, a silly attempt to create some kind of friendship with the woman. Donna returned her gaze to her notepad and scribbled across. The words were impossible for anyone except for Donna to read.

Tracey took a bite of her burrito, her lunch choice from the nearby food truck. As vehicles weren't allowed on the island, this particular "food truck" was attached to a buggy. Horses had clopped it directly up to The Grand Hotel, and film workers had scampered toward it like moths to a flame. Twelve-hour days made teams hungry. That was for sure.

On the far end of The Grand Hotel grounds, Malcolm remained hard at work, standing over a monitor with three other people around him. One of them, Tracey now realized, was Elise, the screenwriter. Elise had mentioned that she would be off and on set, as needed, with hopes to have a "final say" on some of the story choices.

Malcolm and Elise seemed to be in the midst of a heated conversation. Malcolm lifted the screenplay, rolled it up, and smacked his thigh. Elise looked volatile. But after another moment, Elise's familiar smile burst to the surface. Malcolm, too, began to laugh. Tracey arched her brow, then eyed Donna. But Donna remained hard at work, her quesadilla hardly touched. Tracey took another bite of her burrito. It would be another eight hours till she was allowed offset. She had to make this burrito count.

* * *

That night, Tracey limped back to her little house. Her phone was dead. Her legs ached, and although she'd been allowed a few times to use her creativity on set that day, she was beginning to second-guess the decision to work on the film at all. It wasn't just hard work; it was also a collection of egotistical individuals who all assumed their opinion was always correct. Tracey, an island girl through and through, resented anyone like that.

When Tracey opened the front door, she was fixated on a single thing: the tub of ice cream in the freezer. But instead, four figures sprung out from behind the couch, calling out, "Congratulations!"

Tracey yelped and stepped back. Emma, Megan, Elise, and Cindy stood before her, grinning. Cindy had a bottle of champagne lifted, which she opened with a flourish. Bubbles flowed over the top of the bottle and her knuckles.

"What is all this about?" Tracey asked, forcing her voice to be more upbeat than she felt.

"You just finished your first week on set!" Elise called, stepping around the couch to throw her arms around Tracey. "I watched you from afar. You were killing it out there."

Tracey groaned into Elise's shoulder.

"What?" Elise asked, wide-eyed. Her smile faltered.

"Oh, nothing. I just couldn't help but feel like everything I did was wrong," Tracey said with a shrug.

Elise waved a hand. "That's natural for your first week. Everyone told me that Donna was very pleased with your work."

Tracey had to conceal her laughter. Cindy returned soon after with five glasses and poured out the champagne as Megan chatted about how she and Emma couldn't wait to get out on set the next week. Tracey's heart swelled with love for these people, along with the welcome news that the cold-hearted Donna had actually appreciated her.

"A toast!" Cindy said, lifting her glass. "To the best damn costume designer in all the land."

"Assistant costume designer," Tracey corrected.

"Oh, whatever. They couldn't do it without you," Elise said. "Drink up!"

Tracey dropped her head back; the bubbles traced her tongue and lifted her mood.

"Pizzas on its way!" Emma announced, throwing an arm around her mother's shoulder.

"You're spoiling me," Tracey replied, wincing as another pain spiked through her leg.

"Get this lady over to the couch," Elise ordered. "She's been on her feet all day long."

Tracey collapsed on the couch next to her daughter, propped her feet up on the footrest, and listened to the nourishing sound of the women she loved the most in conversation.

"So, what's the scene we're working on next week?" Megan asked brightly, tossing the question out for both Tracey and Elise.

"I think it's the Lilac Festival Scene," Elise replied contemplatively. "From the seventies. Correct me if I'm wrong, Trace."

"That sounds right," Tracey nodded in agreement. "Although if you'd told me the Earth was flat right now, I'd say that sounds right, too."

Elise laughed. "The set makes your head spin."

"You're darn right it does." Tracey sipped more champagne, then added, "I saw you talking to the director this afternoon."

Elise cringed. "Ah. Malcolm Ritter."

"So, you're familiar with him?"

"You've probably heard he was pretty big in Hollywood a few years ago. People were saying his name alongside other big-time director names. And then I heard one day that he backed out of production right before filming. The studio scrambled to fill his director chair," Elise said.

"And you don't know what happened?" Emma asked.

Elise shook her head. "Nobody does. That's a rare thing in Hollywood. Usually, gossip flows fast."

"He's so angry," Tracey offered, her shoulders falling forward. "All the time."

"You shouldn't let his arrogance get in the way of you doing a good job," Elise affirmed, her eyes flashing. "He's insecure about his decision to step away and come back like this. He's probably just having to relearn the ropes. Because you're just now learning the ropes yourself, it makes sense that you'd butt heads."

The pizza arrived soon after. Tracey tried her best to bubble along with Elise, Megan, and Emma's conversations. Mid-way through her first slice, Penny arrived from yet another reckless beach party, describing her newfound love for a dock-worker named Steve.

"He's not like California boys," she told them dreamily as she took a pizza slice. "He listens. He cares."

Megan and Emma locked eyes knowingly. Tracey opened her lips, suddenly overwhelmed with the desire to tell the four of them about her long-ago affair with a sailor named Joey. *But what good would that do?*

"This island. It makes people fall in love," Elise said, shaking her head. She took a small bite of cheese pizza and gave Tracey a tentative smile.

Tracey could practically hear Elise's thoughts, telling her that it was Tracey's "time." But Tracey had been doing just fine alone. Hadn't she?

The night continued on until Tracey's near-constant yawns indicated that she needed a good twelve hours of sleep. One after another, Elise, Penny, Emma, and Megan stood up, gathered the trash and dirty plates, cleaned up the kitchen, and then hugged Tracey goodbye. Emma's hug lasted a little bit longer than the others, which allowed Emma to whisper, "Don't be hard on yourself. This was only your first week."

Tracey groaned and gave her daughter a soft smile. "I hope you're right."

Emma cocked her head. "When have I ever been wrong?"

To this, both Tracey and Emma cackled. Emma gathered her jacket and slung it over her shoulders, laced her arm through Megan's, and padded out the door. Elise and Penny waved before parading their way back to Wayne's for the night.

On the couch in the silence of her little house, Tracey felt hollow. She shifted her legs to the far end of the couch, allowing the cushions to cradle her. For a long time, she focused on her breathing, staring at the ceiling.

And then came a sound that Tracey had come to rely on.

Her phone buzzed.

Tracey reached for her cell on the coffee table. Her heart pounded, a reminder she was alive, so alive, and so ready to feel whatever it was she was about to feel. She then opened the message from Joey and felt her soul rise out of her ears.

JOEY: Do you ever think about what would have happened if we'd stayed together?

Tracey closed her eyes. Devastation took hold of her. If she hadn't been so exhausted, she would have burst into tears.

But Joey wasn't done.

JOEY: My life didn't exactly turn out the way I'd hoped. I found myself going through the motions— becoming a pilot, getting married, having first one child, then another, and then another. I now feel like a stranger in my own life, as though I didn't actually make any of these decisions myself. It's difficult to explain.

JOEY: We were just so stupid and young, Trace. We had no idea what we had.

Tears fell in rivers down her cheeks. Tracey had no idea what to say. She didn't want to put herself in the vulnerable position of agreeing with him. And, above all, she didn't want to tell him that she'd gone ahead and had his baby without telling him.

It would frighten him. And it could enrage him. Tracey didn't want either. Just then, during this moment of weakness, she wanted his attention, his friendship, and whatever love he could give.

TRACEY: You're right about one thing. We had no idea what we had.

TRACEY: But time has passed.

JOEY: Maybe it's not too late.

Tracey's heart seized. She leaped from the couch and flung her phone to the cushion, terrified of the words staring back at her. *What on earth did he mean? They couldn't do anything about this. This was merely a fantasy, something to take up space in their minds. Wasn't it?*

Tracey abandoned her phone, stripping off her clothes as she padded to her bedroom and crawled beneath the sheets. For a long while, she stared into the darkness, her heart thudding. Finally, she slipped into sleep, grateful for a full nine hours away from her reckless thoughts and her aching muscles.

It didn't matter what Joey wrote. She had to remind herself of this, over and over again. They were happier apart. It was just fact.

Wasn't it?

Chapter Ten

"Who is my character? What does she want? What does she need?" Emma spoke with her fists in front of her chest, her eyes to the eggshell blue sky above. She wore only a camisole and a pair of shorts, standing before the massive collection of extra costumes that Tracey and Donna had painstakingly selected for that day's scene at "The Lilac Festival, 1979."

"Calm down, Meryl Streep," Tracey teased. "You're just an extra."

Emma's eyes flashed knowingly. "Behind every extra is a name, a story, heartaches, and fears. Even if the camera is only on me for two seconds, I want the viewers to feel that story."

"Oh my God. You're ridiculous." Megan stood beside her, wiggling into a seventies-style pair of bell bottoms and a white peasant-style shirt, which had also been quite popular on the island in the seventies.

Emma giggled, knowing full well how ridiculous she sounded. Tracey tossed her head back, bubbling with laughter. It was only eight in the morning on the first day of a fresh new week. Around them, other members of the film crew strutted around, setting up lighting equipment, sound equipment, and cameras. Prior to Emma and Megan's arrival, Tracey had already dressed twenty-five extras, who all waited, bored, off to the side. Only Emma gave Tracey any grief about her outfit choice. Tracey supposed this was fitting.

For "Lilac Festival, 1979," the film had sequestered off an entire street in downtown Mackinac Island. For the following ten hours, nobody was allowed to walk up or down the street without the knowledge of the film crew itself. On the far end of the street, tourists and islanders alike stood with coffees lifted, watching the festivities. From afar, it probably looked incredible and strange. Up close, it was just about as stressful as ever.

But Tracey tried to shove those thoughts from her mind.

Together, Tracey and Emma selected a short skirt and a poofy belly shirt for Emma's "character." After dressing, she flipped her hair in the mirror, twisting to the right and left to inspect her form.

Donna bolted past, on her way somewhere important. Upon seeing Emma, however, she stopped short and gave Emma a once-over. "I like that, Tracey," Donna said, giving a rare compliment. "It suits her and the scene incredibly well. Good work."

Tracey could have floated into the heavens above.

The set decorators had created a near picture-perfect scene from the Lilac Festival in 1979, using records from the Mackinac Island Public Library and imitating old photographs. From one stretch of buildings to another, they'd hung a banner that read: **LILAC FESTIVAL 1979**. Below, little food kiosks sold beer, pretzels, sandwiches, lemonade, cakes, and muffins. It hadn't been decided which of the extras would be behind each of these stalls. Tracey knew already that Emma was hungry for this "more pivotal" role.

One of the assistant directors approached the cast of extras, tapping his pen against his clipboard. Emma and Megan pushed their way to the front of the extras, hoping to be noticed. Tracey half-watched, half-kept herself busy with other tasks. She knew that if she dallied for only a second, Donna would approach her and reprimand her. Or worse— the director himself.

It was almost like being back in school again, frightened of detention.

"I need several 'special' extras for today's shoot," the assistant director informed them. "First off, I need a woman for the cake stall."

Several women, including Emma and Megan, flailed their arms around. Unfortunately, the assistant director pointed to an older woman near the back. Admittedly, this woman did seem more "appropriate" for the role of "cake seller."

The assistant director went on, assigning roles for pretzel seller, fudge maker, and clothing retailer. Each time, he seemed to ignore Megan and Emma as though they didn't exist at all.

Until finally, the assistant director arrived at the roles of: "Two women at the beer counter. Both in their twenties. Anyone?"

Tracey smirked, watching as Megan and Emma easily slid into their roles— high-fiving as the assistant director ordered them where to stand, how to pour the beer from the keg (which looked real, from where Tracey stood), and how to speak to customers to ensure that they were still "in the shot." From behind the counter of the fake beer kiosk, Emma waved like a child and jumped up and down with Megan.

"All right, everyone. Quiet on the set." Malcolm stood from his director chair and grimaced at the thirty-plus extras and three members of the main cast. "For those of you not from Mackinac Island, the Lilac Festival is an incredibly important event in the history of Mackinac. Remember, you're meant to feel the magic of this festival that only comes around one time per year. I need to see that joy on your faces. I need it to come through the camera."

The first take began. The director cut it off early, angry with one of the main actresses for skipping a line. He smoothed his hair with his hands and breathed out, saying, "Okay. Okay. Let's take it from the top." But again, the same actress made the same mistake, as though something in her psyche refused to let the mistake go.

Tracey and Donna locked eyes. After a split second, they rushed through the team of extras and actors, fixing their outfits before hustling back to the sidelines. Immediately after they arrived, the director set the shot and said, "ACTION."

It would be a long day. Sweat traced Tracey's neckline and dribbled down her back. Donna seemed unable to sweat; perhaps she'd gotten those glands removed. Tracey had read that California people loved doing insane things like that to their bodies.

That said, she would have done anything not to feel like a sweating cow right then.

They continued on— from one take to the next. Eventually, the director set up a brand-new scene, but with similar players. This particular scene brought the camera closer to the beer kiosk, which thrilled Megan and Emma. You could see the awe playing out across their faces. Just as they'd been taught, they poured beer from kegs into beer bottles, chatting in a make-believe way to the guests as they approached.

Several times between takes, Tracey hustled over to Megan and Emma to adjust their shirts and make sure they hadn't been dribbled with any beer. The first time, Emma muttered, "How are we doing, Mom?"

"I think you'll be up for an Oscar this year. Both of you," Tracey returned.

That scene moved to another. With the camera further back, more extras were in the scene. This meant more attention, all the time. Tracey blinked out across a street that she'd walked down every single day of her life. It all felt so unreal.

Because of this enhanced attention on the other extras, however, Tracey didn't notice Emma's reddening puffy cheeks, or the sweat that stuck to her face. The first time she noticed anything amiss, Emma gripped the side of the beer kiosk and wavered, as though she was about to collapse. Megan muttered something to Emma, and Emma just shook her head in response, clearly terrified and unable to speak.

The director was setting up the shot again. Tracey remained captivated with her daughter. It was like watching a car accident. The timing couldn't have been worse. Just as Malcolm cried, "Action!" Emma rushed out from behind the beer stall, sprinting like Tracey had never seen her sprint. She disappeared into a porta-potty, leaving the rest of the film crew stunned.

"Stop! Stop everything!" Malcolm was furious. He flailed his hands toward Megan, who looked just as confused as everyone else. "What's gotten into your partner over there?" he asked Megan.

Megan just shook her head.

But Tracey couldn't wait around for something to happen. This was her daughter, dammit. Determined, she marched around the camera equipment and rounded toward the other side of the street, where Emma remained in a porta-potty. Aware that everyone in the film crew watched her, Tracey rapped on the soft green door and whispered, "Are you okay, honey?"

It was clear that Emma was quite sick. She moaned and spoke softly. "I'm so sorry, Mom."

"Honey, you don't have to apologize for being sick."

"I just ruined the shoot," Emma whispered.

Tracey spoke so quietly. "Honey, that man has taken so many gosh-darn takes. I think he'll find something that works."

But suddenly, that terrible, dominant voice was far closer to Tracey than ever. "Excuse me? Do you mind telling me why you've held up filming? Do you know how much money we lose every minute that we wait around like this?"

Tracey turned and glared at him. When they locked eyes, Malcolm's cheek twitched.

"Oh. It's you again. Tell me, Costuming Assistant. Why are you always holding up my shoots?" Malcolm demanded.

Tracey's jaw dropped. She felt demeaned, unappreciated, and humiliated. Far behind Malcolm, Donna stood, waving her hands back and forth furiously. Tracey sensed what she meant: "*Don't escalate it.*" But how could Tracey just take this man's abuse lying down?

"Excuse me? Did you not just see her run off set? Clearly, there's something very wrong! Something that has nothing to do with your stupid movie schedule!" Tracey howled.

Donna dropped her chin to her chest. In her eyes, all was lost. Tracey had officially humiliated herself.

But Tracey didn't care at all. In fact, as Malcolm's face twisted and contorted, a result of the rage he felt toward her, Tracey developed a fire all on her own. What Malcolm didn't understand was that the power of an angry mother rivaled any movie director, any warmonger, or any volatile chef.

"That's my daughter in there," Tracey barked. "I don't care what you think or what you do or what you say. I'm going to stand here and make sure she's okay. Your movie can make do without us, for now."

To Tracey's surprise, Malcolm pulled his twisted face around and stalked off. He waved a finger through the air, calling for the film to set up a brand-new scene. After seven or eight takes of the last scene, Malcolm had decided that enough was enough. He'd decided, in a word, to "listen."

Tracey remained next to the porta-potty with her arms clenched tightly over her chest. Although Donna was in the throes of panic on the other side of the street, she occasionally locked eyes with Tracey, gobsmacked. Soon after, a text rang through Tracey's phone from Donna herself.

DONNA: I can't believe he didn't tear your head off.

DONNA: Compassion isn't something I necessarily associate with men like Malcolm.

DONNA: Kudos to your achievements today—both on and off the set. Take your daughter home. Care for her. You'll be needed on set bright and early tomorrow. Don't you forget it.

Tracey, who already half-believed that Donna was on the verge of firing her, held the phone against her chest. She wavered from foot to foot, overwhelmed with emotion. Just then, the porta-potty seemed to spit Emma out.

Just as she'd been immediately before her dash to the bathroom, Emma looked haggard and green. She stretched her hands over her stomach and bit her lip.

"I caused a lot of drama today, didn't I?"

Tracey grimaced. "Don't think anything about it. It's not like you threw up all over their precious film equipment."

Emma scrunched her nose, eyeing the thirty extras and the thirty-plus film cast members, all of whom had witnessed her breakdown. Embarrassment crawled up her face.

"Hey." Tracey interrupted Emma's racing thoughts. "I've been cleared the rest of the day. Why don't we go home, close all the curtains, turn on the AC full blast, watch some reality TV, and eat some soup?"

Emma's eyelids fluttered. "I'd like that. More than I even knew it was possible to like something."

Tracey grabbed her backpack, gave Donna a firm wave, and placed her hand at the base of Emma's back. Together, they trekked up the hill to the home they'd once shared— a world safe from the anger and attitude of strangers and idiots.

Chapter Eleven

Against all of Tracey's best instincts, the following day on set went as scheduled— without a single abusive comment from the director himself. How about that!

The set itself was along the waterline on the other side of the island. Donna and Tracey shared a horse and buggy while discussing the costumes for the scenes that day, which included a beach "love" scene— one that made Donna giggle like a teenager.

"Oh, but the beach! I get that it's romantic," Donna said, making several notes on her list. "But all that sand is disgusting. I would never!"

Tracey, who'd been born on the island and had her share of experiences, just giggled. What Donna didn't know wouldn't hurt her.

"I have to say, I've never arrived to set with a horse and buggy before," Donna said, lifting her chin for a moment of sincere pleasure. The wind off the Straits of Mackinac flowed through her cropped hair, which had grown more accustomed to the Midwestern humidity since her arrival two weeks before. "There's a magic to it. It's like going back in time."

"Try growing up here," Tracey said. "You think this is how the whole world must work. But going off the island means going forward in time, and it's not always so comfortable."

Donna's eyes widened. "I'd imagine not."

The day went well, perhaps better than it should have. Tracey worked like a machine, hopping from one end of the set to the other, fetching bobby pins and assisting with clean-up and racking and re-racking clothing carts until her head spun.

At eight p.m. that night, Malcolm announced they were finished for the day, Tracey breathed a heavy sigh of relief. She grabbed her water and downed half of it, suddenly conscious of how dehydrated she was. When she lifted her eyes again, she discovered that one of the assistant directors had taken the microphone from Malcolm to make another announcement.

"Hello, everyone. This marks two weeks of incredible and intense work here on Mackinac Island," the assistant director began. "And for this reason, we've arranged a little party, right here on the beach. Starting now!" He raised a hand excitedly. "Give yourselves a round of applause. And let loose!"

The film crew and actors eyed one another curiously and clapped sporadically. With how hard they'd been working, there hadn't been a "party" vibe to the set thus far. But just a few minutes later, several horse and buggies arrived, carrying kegs, or attached to food kiosks that advertised tacos, burritos, pizzas, and fried chicken.

"How about that..." Tracey was still hard at work beside Donna, who also muttered with disbelief. "Will any of us find the energy for something like this?"

Donna scoffed. "You don't think we have the energy for a party? You clearly haven't been in the film industry long."

Tracey laughed, grateful any time that Donna chose to tell a joke, even if it was slightly insulting.

"Okay. Okay. I'll stick around," Tracey said.

Within the next half-hour, the clothing racks and film equipment had been sent back to the nearby warehouses, leaving the film crew and the actors and actresses to crack open beers, sip cocktails, and bob around to the beat that boomed from the stereo system. Tracey stood awkwardly next to several extras, chatting with them about where they were from and how they'd gotten involved in the film in the first place. Had she known that there was a party, she would have invited Emma along as a sort of social crutch.

"I have to run to the bathroom," Tracey told one of the extras, who barely registered that she'd spoken.

Tracey turned toward the porta-potties and shifted through her purse to find her phone. There, she found two brand-new messages from Joey. Her heart skipped a beat.

JOEY: I flew from Santa Fe to Nashville. It's so hot. Steaming. Wish I was on that gorgeous island of yours.

JOEY: I remember the water there. So turquoise, like the Mediterranean.

Tracey wrote back, grateful to have someone there at the party with her, even if he was "a secret."

TRACEY: I'm at a film party. It's filled with beautiful people, and I have no idea what to do with myself.

TRACEY: I wish you were on Mackinac, too. The lake awaits you. :)

"Hey! Tracey!" A voice pulled Tracey out of her reverie. She turned to find Elise walking toward her, wearing a gorgeous white dress with a plunging neckline. Behind her, Wayne waved, drinking a beer.

"Hi!" Tracey shoved her phone back into her purse and

wrapped her arms around her half-sister. "I didn't know you were coming!"

Elise nodded. "They told me a few days ago. It was supposed to be a surprise." Her eyes flashed back toward the party, where everyone had collected themselves into separate groups— the lighting people and the sound people and the extras and the higher-ups. "It's really cliquey, isn't it? Like high school all over again."

"I already felt like the odd one out," Tracey confessed.

"Well, I'm here now. We can have our own fun. Do you want to grab a drink and dance with me? I have an eye on that taco stand, but I want to move my body around first. Come on!"

Tracey followed after Elise, laughing as she dropped her purse off to the side and allowed her arms and legs to flow freely in time with the music. Elise was a good dancer, better than she should have been. Tracey tried to both imitate her and come up with her own dance moves, alternating between feeling like a fool and then feeling like an even bigger fool. Such was the way of being in her mid-forties.

Above them, a Mackinac Moon bloomed, hearty and milky white over the lake. Tracey's heart crackled at the sight. How many times had she seen the moon over the island? How many times had its beauty broken her heart?

When they finished their drinks, they lined up for another. Several members of the film crew approached, excited to chat with Elise, the screenwriter. It was clear that they were in awe of her success, but all hungry for their own. They wanted to know how she'd managed it. Elise was gracious, telling them that, although she had worked very hard, she knew that she "got lucky" in a lot of ways.

"If you have a story to tell, all you can do is sit down at your computer and start typing," she told a twenty-something who worked for the lighting department. "Nobody really needs your story, you know? But once they have it in their lives, maybe it will change everything."

The twenty-something's eyes caught the light of the brewing bonfire, which sputtered toward the sky hungrily. Beside Elise, Tracey shifted her weight nervously. After the twenty-something grabbed her own drink and headed off to hang with the rest of the lighting department, Elise turned to Tracey and puffed out her cheeks.

"I never know what to tell people who are looking for advice."

"It sounded really good to me," Tracey said.

Elise sighed, furrowing her brow. "You think?" After another pause, she added, "I'm sure you'll be right there with me in a few years, giving advice right and left as you work your way higher and higher in the Hollywood costuming food chain."

Tracey held back a snort. "I don't know about that."

Elise's face was quizzical. "Everyone tells me what a marvelous job you're doing. You're empathetic with the extras; you stand up to the director when you have to, and you actually make Donna laugh. Not an easy feat."

Tracey giggled. They'd reached the bartender, who mixed them up two gin and tonics. As Elise reached for hers, Wayne approached from behind, wrapping his arms around her waist and kissing her neck. Tracey sipped her drink, closing her eyes as Wayne and Elise shared intimate whispers that she couldn't hear.

Tracey forced herself through the next half-hour, masquerading as a woman who knew how to have fun at a party, even when she felt like an alien. She danced briefly with the lighting crew, ate a taco next to Donna (who complained about the spices on the meat the entire time), and warmed her feet at the bonfire, listening to a young couple bicker about whether or not their relationship would extend beyond the film shoot.

Had Tracey and Joey had similar conversations about the nature of their relationship? Tracey couldn't remember any. Back then, she'd been exceedingly coy, pretending not to care about the things that made her heart burst.

Speaking of. *Had he written anything back?* Tracey hopped up from the bonfire to find her purse along the side of the dance floor. Sure enough, Joey had written her— words that sizzled with drama.

It was as though their souls were aligned.

JOEY: When I flew home from Santa Fe, I wanted to try to make things work with my wife. It's what you're told to do, you know. There's so much pressure on the institution of marriage. But when I entered the door, she started to dig into me. She demanded more of me than I could possibly give after such an intense flight schedule.

JOEY: I hope this isn't too much to tell you. I mean, I feel so alone. Like I have no one to talk to about any of this. When I got married and had children, I never imagined I'd lose most of my friendships along with it.

TRACEY: You can talk to me about this.

In truth, it felt remarkable to be his sounding board. It had been a long time since a man had trusted Tracey with his innermost thoughts.

JOEY: Thank you, Tracey. It means so much.

JOEY: I feel that my wife is jealous of my career and pushing me away because of it.

JOEY: But it's how I put food on the table for her, and for our children. It's like— I'm either thousands and thousands of feet in the air, or I'm

at home, feeling tormented and alone. Neither feels entirely good all the time, but I'd take being in the air over being at home any day of the week.

As Tracey read and responded to Joey's messages, she wandered through the shadows of the beach. In time, the party behind her seemed like someone else's dream. The cacophony of laughter echoed out across the water. She felt she'd never been a part of it.

But just as she began to scribe another message to Joey, she heard something coming directly from the darkness in front of her. First, it was the crack of a stick; then, a man's voice, thick with passion and in a way, terrified.

Tracey stopped, turned off the light from her phone, and listened intently.

"I just don't understand. Why can't you put her on the phone? Please?" The man's voice rose out of the darkness. As Tracey's eyes adjusted, she could make out a broad-shouldered man, his hand whipping through his hair as he paced.

"I understand that," the man continued, sounding more and more desperate. "Don't you know I understand that? But I just need it. Please. Put her on. I just want to hear her voice."

With a funny jolt, Tracey realized— this wasn't just any voice; this wasn't just any man. This was Malcolm Ritter, the once-renowned director. He no longer sounded strong and powerful, on the verge of ripping her head off on set. Instead, he sounded broken, defeated, like a man on his last leg, begging for his own survival.

Slowly, Tracey backed away from Malcolm. She felt privy to information that felt too intimate. Before he could notice her, she turned on her heel and sped back toward the bonfire, her heart pounding. When she reached it, she found Wayne and Elise, cocktails lifted, bantering easily.

"We were wondering where you'd run off to!" Elise sounded bright, perhaps slightly tipsy.

Tracey wrapped a strand of hair around her ear. "I think I might head back downtown."

"So soon?" Elise sounded disappointed.

Tracey nodded. "Twelve-hour days are nothing to scoff at."

Elise directed Tracey toward a line-up of carriages, which were leaving every thirty minutes to take people back to the other side of the island. Tracey leaped on the next carriage, dropping her head back on the headrest as the man who drove the carriage whistled his own rendition of "A Foggy Day (In London Town)." Everything about the night felt surreal. It was time for Tracey to stop the nightmare in its tracks.

Chapter Twelve

Tracey scrambled through her purse to find her house key. The carriage ride had sobered her all the way up, but her muscles continued to scream from the long hours on set, and her eyes seemed to blur the world around her, making everything like an impressionist painting.

To Tracey's surprise, several lights remained on in the house— the light over the kitchen table, the light in the hallway, and a lamp next to the couch. This wasn't like her. Tracey was ordinarily very environmentally conscious, grateful for what the Earth offered her. She hoped that they could keep it going for hundreds of years longer. Tracey clicked off the lights, one after another, until she reached her bedroom and discovered the actual reason for the lights being on.

There, burrowed under a number of blankets and propped up on several of Tracey's fluffiest pillows, was her daughter, Emma. On the far wall, their favorite reality TV channel played from Tracey's television. On the bedside table sat a half-eaten bowl of popcorn and a Diet Coke, Emma's ultimate comfort food.

It had been a long time since Emma had climbed into Tracey's bed for comfort.

"Hi, honey." Tracey stepped into the bluish shadows of the room, which was only illuminated by the TV.

Emma tilted her head just so. The light from the TV caught against her tear-soaked face. Tracey's lips parted with surprise.

Immediately, her head spun with potential reasons for this sorrow. The first and most obvious reason, she knew, had to do with Megan's decision to head off to college, while Emma would remain on the island, without a single clue of what to do with her life next. This sort of aimlessness could feel very stark and very lonely. Tracey remembered it well.

Tracey sat at the edge of the bed and gripped her daughter's hand. Emma sniffled.

"This is a surprise," Tracey finally said as a way to break the silence.

Emma looked as though she wanted to smile but failed. She sniffed again as Tracey glanced back up at the TV.

"I like this one," Tracey said.

"I know. You're obsessed with all the house flipper shows," Emma pointed out.

"It's fascinating!" Tracey pretended to glance around the bedroom. "We should really re-do our entire house sometime. You and me. A big project."

Emma grimaced. She reached for a handful of popcorn and ate it slowly, chewing on each puffy morsel a little too long.

"I didn't expect you so late," Emma said, ignoring Tracey's idea about redoing the house.

"They had a surprise party for us on the beach. It wasn't exactly a welcome surprise, either. I was exhausted." Tracey considered telling Emma about Malcolm, about the sorrow in his voice. But verbalizing it seemed almost too catty.

Emma nodded, her brow furrowing. And then, after

another long pause, she wailed like a child. Her face was tomato-red and passionate.

"Emma!" Tracey was overwhelmed. She scrambled deeper onto the bed and wrapped her arms around her daughter, holding her until the wails stopped. "Honey, it's okay. Really. Whatever it is, we can find a way through it."

Emma quivered against her. Tracey smoothed her hair, hunting for the perfect thing to say. "Honey, if this is about Megan..."

Emma twisted her neck and gave her mother a quizzical look. "What?"

Tracey stuttered. "Isn't this about Megan heading to college?"

Emma made a soft noise in her throat. "Oh, that." She shrugged. "I'm not exactly thrilled that she's leaving. But it's not like I thought we would work at the fudge shop for the rest of our lives."

"Okay." Tracey shook her head slightly. "Then what is it?"

Emma burrowed her head into her mother's shoulder. "I have no idea how to tell you."

"If you can't tell me, then who can you tell?"

Emma's laughter was edged with sadness. "I haven't told anyone. It's been my secret for so long."

Tracey lifted her head back, locking eyes with Emma. Her stomach twisted with recognition.

"You were so sick on set. It came on so spontaneously..." Tracey whispered.

Emma nodded. "Yes. But it wasn't the first time that's happened. I'm just normally able to hide it a whole lot better."

"Oh my God. You're..."

Emma's lips curved toward her ears. The smile was knowing, without the slightest hint of happiness.

"Pregnant. Yes." Emma's cheeks tightened to reveal her dimples.

Tracey's heart split in two. She was reminded of that long-ago day when she'd confessed her own pregnancy to her mother, Mandy. Joey had been long-gone, no more than a figment of her imagination at that point. Mandy had taken one look at her and said—

"You're going to be okay. You aren't alone. We can do this together." Tracey said it to her daughter now. She felt as though Mandy spoke through her.

But again, Emma burst into tears. The intensity was too much for her to bear.

"Oh, honey. Honey." Tracey held onto her, rocking back and forth until the tears lost their strength. "How long have you known?"

"I found out six weeks ago," Emma breathed. "But last week, the doctor said I'm already about three months along."

"Three months!" Tracey's heart cracked. "You've been carrying this secret that whole time? And you went to the doctor by yourself?"

Emma winced. "I couldn't make up my mind about what to do. Around the time that I took the first pregnancy test, my on-again, off-again relationship with Grant, the guy in question, became officially 'off' again. He then left the island, telling me that he would call. I couldn't bring myself to tell him about the pregnancy. I didn't want to force him into any fatherhood role that he didn't feel ready for."

It was almost exactly what Tracey had said about Joey.

Life had a way of repeating itself.

Emma burrowed herself deeper into Tracey's pillows. Tracey bit hard on her tongue, searching for something to say. *How she loved this girl! How she wanted to make everything all right again!*

"Do you think I should tell him? About the pregnancy?" Emma asked, her eyes on the TV.

"I think you should at least give him the option of stepping up," Tracey said softly.

This was a contrast to her life (or lack thereof) with Joey. She hadn't had a way to contact him about Emma's birth. Otherwise, perhaps she would have.

"He's just so selfish. I don't know if I want to be reminded of how selfish he is," Emma breathed. "When he was selfish within the bounds of our relationship, it sucked. But if his behavior hurts our son or daughter? I won't be able to forgive him."

Tracey blinked back tears. She laced her fingers through Emma's and whispered, "You don't have to decide anything right now."

"I told myself I didn't have to decide anything for the past six weeks," Emma countered. "I went along with my life, pretending like the baby wasn't happening. But boy, is this baby happening."

Tracey tilted her head, remembering the glasses of champagne she'd poured, the wine nights they'd had. As her lips parted, Emma shook her head, as though she could read her mother's mind.

"I didn't touch a drop of alcohol after I found out," she said. "I thought you would notice and ask me what the heck was going on. But you didn't!"

Tracey laughed and shook her head. "Now, I'm the selfish one. I've been so bogged down with this newfound film career. I haven't paid attention to what's actually in front of me. I'm sorry, Emma."

"It was for the best. I needed to wrap my mind around it," Emma told her. "But when you stood up for me the other day on set? I realized that you would stand up for me and my baby every step of the way. And I realized I really, really needed that support."

Tracey's eyes filled with tears. She burrowed herself in the pillows alongside her daughter, holding the silence for a long time.

"God," Emma said suddenly, pointing to the television. "Are they really going to paint that bathroom lavender?"

Tracey shuddered with laughter. She'd hardly noticed the reality TV show at all.

"It's hideous," Tracey agreed. "What would you go with?"

"Um. Anything else. It's such a tiny space. It's going to feel too cutesy," Emma said. She placed her hand tenderly over her stomach, a move Tracey had never seen her do.

Somehow, this protective move made Emma look all the more like a mother.

Somehow, this instilled this reality in Tracey's mind.

This was really happening.

Tracey and Emma continued to banter about the reality TV show deep into the night. Just before Emma drifted off to sleep, she whispered that she had a doctor's appointment soon, that she wanted her mother there by her side. Tracey said, "There's nowhere else in the world I'd rather be."

With Emma fast asleep and tucked deep beneath the blankets of Tracey's bed, Tracey turned off the television and tiptoed to the bathroom, where she washed her face and applied lotion.

Her eyes on herself in the mirror, a strange voice in the back of her mind told her: "This is a good thing. Emma will remain on the island, close to you, forever."

But there was sorrow in getting exactly what you wanted. Tracey would have done anything to keep Emma on the island forever. But a surprise pregnancy with a man you couldn't trust to be a father? She wouldn't have wished that on her daughter. She wouldn't have wished that on anyone.

Back in the kitchen, Tracey poured herself a glass of water and hunted through her purse for her phone. All this talk about surprise pregnancies and inadequate fathers had cast her deep into her own nostalgia.

She had to hear from Joey. She had to hear his voice in her head (even if that voice was just something she'd recreated based on very old memories).

Sure enough, Joey had written. And the messages were beyond her wildest dreams.

JOEY: Talking to you the past few weeks has renewed my faith in humanity. Thank you.

JOEY: I have to admit— I'm so curious to see you in person.

Tracey sniffed, her head pounding. Did she actually dare to walk down this road?

TRACEY: I'd like to see you, too.

JOEY: How about tomorrow? Dinner?

Tracey snorted. Her instincts told her to throw her phone across the room.

TRACEY: How on earth could you manage that?

JOEY: :)

JOEY: You forget. I'm a pilot. Quick travel isn't exactly a difficult thing for me.

JOEY: Don't say no.

JOEY: You'd break my heart.

Chapter Thirteen

Joey Gilbert was coming to Mackinac Island. The thought rang through Tracey's head the moment she awoke like an impossibly loud gong. She staggered to the bathroom and scalded herself beneath a hot shower, trying to make sense of any of this. Emma was pregnant; Joey wanted to return to Tracey's life; neither father nor daughter knew about the other and existed in two very secret worlds. *How could she ever bridge the divide?*

It was seven in the morning, a blissful Saturday in July. Sunlight glittered through the separation between the soft drapes in the kitchen. Tracey stood with a mug of coffee, disassociating as she gazed outside. Her confusion was slowly replaced with panic. Although, yes, she and Joey had seen one another briefly at the airport— she wanted to make a lasting impression, the sort that made her ex-lover think, "Damn. I messed up when I left that woman behind."

It was only human to feel this way.

It was every woman's heartache to ask, before any main event, "What the heck am I going to wear?"

Emma remained asleep. She looked so peaceful, her face angelic as she dove through dreamland. Tracey closed the door between the hallway and her bedroom, stuffed her feet into her tennis shoes, and headed out the door. For the first time in several weeks, she made her way to her downtown boutique, which she'd basically closed for the month of filming.

Over the years, Tracey had built up an impressive collection at the boutique itself. It was the most sought-after boutique on Mackinac Island, drawing women together from all walks of life to try on dresses, skirts, blouses, hats, and artisan jewelry. It was Tracey's greatest joy to discuss fashion with the many women who entered the boutique, to ask what their fashion goals were and how they wanted the world to perceive them. It was fascinating to hear their wide range of answers.

Once within the walls of the boutique itself, Tracey filled her lungs with air and immediately felt at peace. Before her was a wide array of hand-selected outfits, all of which had been Tracey-approved. It was the perfect place, then, for Tracey to find something to wear for her reunion with the father of her child.

Over the next hour and a half, Tracey had a mini, one-woman fashion show. She donned turquoise dresses, tan skirts, bulky jewelry, and simple gold bands; she buttoned and unbuttoned blouses, hung and re-hung dresses, and sauntered up and down the boutique in pairs of heels. All the while, her speaker system played music that Emma said: "pumped you up." Tracey could only laugh at herself. She felt like the main character in a movie all about her life.

"Stranger than fiction," she muttered to herself as she shifted her body left and right, eyeing her figure in a dark green dress.

This, her gut told her, was "the one."

Suddenly, a knock rang out from the front door. Tracey

turned around to find a group of women, coffees from The Grind in hand. Their chatter and laughter rang out.

Tracey unlocked the door and peered out. "Hello?"

The blond of the trio said, "Oh, Tracey! It's so good to see you again. We come here every single year for our girls' trip, and we were devastated to see that your boutique was closed. But when I peered in, I saw you in there, and I thought maybe you'd let us peruse your tremendous collection?" She shrugged playfully, like a woman who was used to getting exactly what she wanted.

Tracey was surprised to hear herself say, "Oh, sure. Anything for some of my favorite customers!" She had no idea who these women were, but they clearly remembered her and her "tremendous collection." Their words, not hers.

The three women spent more than an hour within the boutique. Grateful to pour her energy into something other than her anxious thoughts about her ex-lover, Tracey fetched new sizes, gave her opinions about designs and colors, and chatted easily with the shoppers. Several more tourists entered the boutique, grateful for something to do that Saturday morning while their husbands played golf or tennis.

By noon, Tracey realized that she'd already sold an incredible four hundred and thirty dollars in inventory. Overwhelmed and incredibly happy, she texted Cindy the news.

True to form, Cindy was ready to nag her.

CINDY: Why on earth did you open the shop today? You've worked more than sixty hours on set this week! Don't tire yourself out!

Tracey rolled her eyes, shoved her phone into her pocket, and lifted her eyes toward the door. "Have a beautiful day!" she called to a mother-daughter duo who stepped out, swinging their bags of new purchases.

Immediately after they disappeared, someone else filled the space in the doorframe— a six-foot-three hunk of a man who looked very out of place within Tracey's adorable boutique. Trained in the art of customer service, Tracey immediately greeted the man with a "Good morning and welcome!"

But a split second later, she and the man locked eyes, and her heart sank into her stomach.

It was Malcolm Ritter.

What on earth was Malcolm Ritter doing in her boutique?

"Oh. Hi." Tracey blinked several times, trying to maintain her smile.

Malcolm Ritter stepped closer, shoving his hands into the pockets of his black jeans. For the thousandth time, Tracey marveled that a man could wear such stifling jeans in the middle of summer.

"I didn't know you worked here," he said. Did this serve as a "greeting" out in Los Angeles?

"I don't just work here," Tracey told him. "I own the place."

Malcolm's eyes traced the boutique, taking stock of the hats, the jewelry, and the lace-up sandals. As he stepped deeper into the store, the shadows under his eyes became more apparent. He even looked slightly green. Was he hungover from the party the night before?

"I'm staying downtown," he said, lifting a thumb back toward the street. "I kept passing this boutique, sad that it was closed."

Tracey cocked her head. *Why on earth would a big-time director want to investigate her little boutique?*

"I've just been working so hard on the film," Tracey said. "I should hire someone else to keep it going during the day."

She couldn't tell him the truth: that she was even more of a control freak when it came to her boutique than he was as a director.

Malcolm placed his hands on his hips. He no longer looked like a strong and passionate director; he looked timid and frightened, more like the man she'd heard on the phone the night before. What was it he'd said? "I just want to hear her voice." Whose voice had he been talking about?

"Can I help you find anything in particular?" Tracey heard herself ask, just as she would ask any other customer.

Malcolm coughed. It was obvious that he felt embarrassed and awkward. "I need a new dress for a little girl. Age five."

Tracey had a moderate-sized collection of feminine children's clothing. She'd discovered them to be top sellers, with mothers and grandmothers eager to dress their children a bit fancier for vacation dinners. Plus, she adored the little lace and floral designs, allowing herself to fall into the nostalgia of dressing her little girl.

"Over here," Tracey said, directing Malcolm toward the corner. She began to remove some of her favorites: a dark green dress with a sharp white Peter Pan collar; a yellow flower-spotted dress with puffy sleeves; a maroon onesie that buttoned to the top.

"Wow. My ex-wife will adore these," Malcolm said, shaking his head. "I can't think of anywhere out in LA that sells anything quite like these."

Tracey's heart skipped a beat. It felt remarkable, hearing news of an ex-wife and, now, a daughter, all from the cold-hearted director himself.

"I try to buy almost everything from individual sellers," Tracey explained. "I want things to feel unique. Not like another fast-fashion brand."

"It's like you took the words right out of my ex-wife's mouth," Malcolm said. He then spread his arms out on either side of his muscular frame. "I want to buy all three."

Tracey was more than surprised. "Oh. That's fantastic."

"I don't suppose you have a mail service?"

"Of course. I sell almost everything online, as well. It's a way to keep the business going during the quieter months on the island," Tracey explained. "If you want, I can box these up for you, nice and pretty, and send them on their way."

Malcolm wiped a handkerchief across his forehead. Tracey had a hunch it was hangover sweats.

"That would be fantastic," Malcolm breathed.

Tracey grabbed a pad of paper and a pen. "Just fill out the address here." She began to fold the garments tenderly, removing their tags and wrapping them in beautiful tissue paper. After Malcolm finished filling out the address, he brandished his credit card. *What did a famous film director make per year?* Tracey wondered it abstractly. The prices in Los Angeles were exorbitant. She could only imagine his yearly rate.

Just as Tracey reached for the credit card, Malcolm pulled it away. "Before I pay, I want to apologize."

This can't be happening, Tracey thought.

"As you can see, I have a daughter. Just like you." Malcolm's nostrils flared. "When your daughter was sick on set, and you stood up to me, I realized what a monster I'd been. I haven't been sleeping well since."

Tracey was genuinely shocked. "It's really okay."

"It's not," Malcolm told her firmly. "It's not an excuse, but this entire filming process has torn me up inside. I was out of the business for many years and have put tremendous pressure on myself to make this particular film work. I'm so nervous that I'll mess this up, and everything I worked for will mean nothing at all."

Tracey had never imagined that a big-time director could be so in-tune with reality. She swallowed the lump in her throat. Malcolm then slipped the credit card between her fingers and dropped his gaze to the ground. The intensity between them seemed too great.

"You're doing an incredible job," Tracey whispered, her voice wavering. "You shouldn't be so hard on yourself. It seems to come naturally to you."

Malcolm chuckled sadly. "That's the thing. It doesn't come naturally to me at all. Yes, I love it. But sometimes I ask myself, is it worth it?"

The printer buzzed and clicked, producing Malcolm's receipt. Tracey placed it in his hand, locking eyes with him. She knew it wasn't her "duty" to take his pain and sorrow away. She had no idea what his situation was.

"Your daughter will love the dresses," Tracey whispered instead. "I like to think that every piece in my boutique was selected with love."

Malcolm nodded, his eyes still on hers. "I can feel that love and care, both in this boutique and in the way you work on set. Thank you for it." He then padded the top of the garments, which rustled with the tissue paper. "And thank you for sending these off for me. As a guy, I never really figured out how to deal with tissue paper."

Tracey laughed, grateful that he'd broken the tension. He then bowed his head and said, "See you Monday." And with that, he turned on his heel and disappeared into the lush Saturday afternoon light.

Chapter Fourteen

Tracey closed up the boutique at four-thirty and wandered along the boardwalk, watching the sailboats, and falling into the daydream of the gorgeous day. Joey reported that he would leave Nashville around five-thirty, which meant he would land around seven. Tracey's heart skipped every other beat. To steady her mind, she paused at a wine bar and wrote in her journal— mostly anxious thoughts and her innermost desires.

July 16, 2022

I never imagined, not in my wildest dreams, that Joey Gilbert would come back into my life.

The day Emma was born, I wept for Joey and pitied him for missing such a gorgeous moment. There she was, his perfect first child. Where was he on that particular day, I wonder? On a sailboat somewhere, watching the sunset? Driving across the continent, as free as a bird?

Tracey clicked her pen and sipped her wine, her head swimming with fear. Across the wine bar, a young couple sat with their hands touching the table, speaking with intensity.

Tracey had a premonition about the next hours of her life. The previous few weeks of Joey and Tracey's correspondence demanded a similar intensity. *What would they say to one another?*

About an hour before seven, Tracey began her walk up to the Mackinac Island Airport, located just southeast of the Cave of the Woods and not far from the Stonecliff Hotel. Tracey had never flown from the Mackinac Island Airport, as aircraft from the airport didn't tend to go anywhere far. Besides, it wasn't like she ever had anywhere pressing she needed to go.

Tracey walked up the paved road that led to the tiny airport itself, behind which was the runway. She stood in the fading sunshine with her eyes lifted toward the blue sky. Every tiny dot seemed, at first, to be his approaching plane before revealing itself to be only a bird.

Each time, Tracey's stomach stirred with a mix of disappointment and relief. Perhaps Joey would do what Joey did best and "bail." Perhaps then, she could return to her life pre-Joey— a life that had been infinitely less confusing.

About five minutes past seven, however, an aircraft appeared overhead. It was a tiny private plane, the likes of which could support only one pilot and a passenger or two. Tracey felt herself jump up and down like a child, a smile breaking across her cheeks.

From her vantage point, the aircraft made a perfect landing before stopping, wheeling around, and parking in the designated aircraft parking spots located near the building itself. The door lifted to reveal a handsome man wearing a baseball hat, a pair of jeans, and a white t-shirt. He looked like the perfect, All-American man— a man who liked baseball games, barbecues, family reunions, and boundless laughter. As an added bonus, he was also incredibly handsome and had the skills to fly a plane across three states to visit her.

How about that.

When Joey caught sight of her, his smile matched hers. Tracey squealed like a teenager and felt herself run toward him. It was like she'd lost control of her own legs. He started running too, and before Tracey knew it, he'd grabbed her around the waist and lifted her in a circle. Her legs extended out behind her, as did the skirt of her brand-new dress.

His blue eyes were the most captivating things she'd ever seen. His jawline was sharp and stunning. And his smile! It tore her apart.

As he set her back on the pavement, she squealed again and wrapped her arms around him. He hugged her back.

"Tracey Swartz, as I live and breathe," he said quietly, as though he was just as confused about all of this as she was.

Tracey waited for Joey as he checked in his plane with the proper Mackinac Island authorities. His voice was powerful and sure of itself, just as it always had been. She checked her phone a few times, frightened that Emma would demand where she was— or worse, see her out on the town with Joey Gilbert that night.

But instead, Emma texted to say that she planned to tell Megan "the big news" that night.

EMMA: It's finally time to face this head-on.

EMMA: I guess we'll probably just be at our apartment, eating snacks, crying, and watching movies. Join if that sounds like fun!

Tracey laughed.

TRACEY: As much as I'd love to, I have plans tonight. Take care of yourself! And remember that no matter what, Megan and I will be here for you.

TRACEY: We love you and that baby so, so much.

"You ready?" Joey appeared before her, slipping his wallet into his back pocket.

They walked. What else could they possibly do, given the strangeness of the situation and the aimless quality of life? They wandered through the surrounding woods, past the Wawashkamo Golf Course and the Equestrian Center, toward British Landing. Lucky for Tracey, the island could do so much speaking for her, bringing back endless memories from Joey's long-ago "wandering" days.

At first, their conversation was friendly and one-dimensional. Joey told her how the flight had gone, that he'd been grateful to make good time. He told her where else he'd flown that week for work and that he really loved going out to California, that the lifestyle was something he "really aspired to." Tracey told him that she hadn't adored California the way he had, that she wasn't so sure about the vanity of so many of the residents and the high prices of everything.

Joey's eyes glittered. "You're just too kind for a place like that."

"I don't know about that," Tracey shot back.

Joey stopped short. They stood on the beach of British Landing, with the splendor of the lake before them. It was probably eight or eight-thirty, and the sky was gorgeous with purple and pink hues stretching every which way.

"I've been all over the world, Tracey. I've met all kinds of people. Genuine kindness is a rare thing, but it's something you have. I promise you that."

Tracey's cheeks burned. She dropped her gaze to the sand beneath them, where she could track their footsteps back to the tree line behind them.

A sudden thought rang through her: *was she really so "genuinely kind" if she still kept the existence of a daughter from a father and vice versa?*

Joey chuckled, forcing Tracey's eyes back toward his cerulean ones.

"You still don't know how to take a compliment," Joey

teased her. "But hey, I'm starving. Why don't we head back to town and grab a bite to eat? I have a hunch that Mackinac still has some of the best restaurants around."

Tracey's lips twisted into a smile. How could she resist his charms?

"They've only gotten better, I'm afraid," she told him.

"Oh no. Guess I'll have to try them all," Joey returned. He then pressed his hand for a brief moment at the base of her back, guiding her toward the tree line and back toward town.

* * *

The walk back to downtown Mackinac was about two and a half miles. After a spring and summer of early-morning runs, Tracey appreciated the strength of her legs and her firm posture. Joey, too, had kept himself in shape and spoke briefly about a marathon he'd run the previous year in Nashville.

"I always said I hated exercise," he joked as they walked through the fading light.

"I remember," Tracey said. "But what did we know? We were in our twenties. I don't think I even so much as glanced at a vegetable until I hit thirty-two."

This, Tracey knew, was a lie. She'd struggled to get the baby weight off and painstakingly counted calories and forked her way through countless salads.

But Joey appreciated the joke. "I appreciate living as long as I have. If a vegetable or two helps me live a few decades longer, then pass the asparagus. I'm ready."

They reached downtown Mackinac around nine-thirty that night. Perhaps another Mackinac season would have seen the bars and restaurants shuttered for the night, but this deep in July meant one thing and one thing only: Mackinac tourists and residents alike tried to push the summer nights as last as possible.

"Do you still like pizza?" Tracey asked Joey mischievously.

Joey's eyes sparkled. "If I ever stop liking pizza, you can take me to have a lobotomy."

Tracey clutched her stomach and howled with laughter. Her laughter ricocheted from building to building, joining the chaos of forty or fifty conversations just on Main Street alone.

"Actually, that was a test," Tracey said. "To make sure you're the actual Joey Gilbert and not some stand-in."

"Do you have any more tests for me?" Joey asked.

"Not until after pizza," Tracey replied. "I'm not cruel."

The pizza restaurant right off Main Street seated them at the table closest to the water. A steady breeze rushed from the Straits, flinging Tracey's hair behind her shoulders. Joey gazed out across the water, captivated. *How was it possible that he'd seen so much and done so much, yet still found such beauty in little, old Mackinac?*

They ordered two pizzas, one with salami, mushrooms, and onions, and another with black olives, green peppers, eggplant, and an extra sprinkling of feta cheese.

"That sounds delicious," Joey said, rubbing his palms together. "Down in Nashville, everything we eat is meat-meat-meat. I'm excited to try something different."

"I don't mind eating vegetarian now and again," Tracey said. She caught herself before she added, "*my daughter says it's environmentally friendly*."

"I think we live in a world that requires more thought before our actions," Joey agreed, furrowing his brow.

"So different than the old days, huh?" Tracey continued. "All we did was do-do-do, without much think-think-think."

Joey laughed good-naturedly as the waitress returned with a bottle of wine. As she cranked the cork from the top, she smiled down at them and said, "It's such a beautiful night for a bottle of wine."

"It really is!" Joey exuded joy.

"Tracey, where did you find this guy?" the waitress asked with a smile as she poured their glasses.

Tracey stuttered before Joey found the right words to answer.

"She pulled me out of her nightmares," he said mischievously. "Right, Trace?"

Tracey giggled and lifted her glass toward Joey's. "Nah. Just some beautiful memories."

They clinked glasses as the waitress wandered over to another table. Joey held Tracey's eyes for a long time. After a long moment of silence, he added, "And here's to many more memories."

Tracey thought she might fall to the floor with panic.

But after the first sip of French Bordeaux, she rebounded, chatting amicably about the recent film work she'd done on the island and whether or not she saw herself doing it more in the future.

"I can't imagine that they'll film on the island again," Tracey said. "And I don't know if I'd want to leave the island for that kind of work."

"Why not? You could make Mackinac your base and head out to LA every once in a while. We could even meet up there. As I said, I'm always going in and out of the city, and I know all the best restaurants," Joey said. There it was again, that twinkle in his eye.

Tracey's stomach tied itself into knots. Not once had Joey mentioned his wife. This, so soon after him telling her that he had regrets about his marriage, both thrilled and terrified Tracey. *What did it mean? Had he told his wife it was over? Should she ask?*

Don't get ahead of yourself, she thought. *This is just an ex-boyfriend from the past. Nothing more.*

"Maybe," Tracey said.

"Come on. You were obviously made for this line of work,"

Joey pushed.

Tracey sipped her wine and took in the full vision of this man, a man she'd once loved. How could she possibly ask all the questions she wanted to? Questions like: *what happened to you after you left Mackinac? How did you finally clean up your act? Do you want to know about your actual first child?*

But instead, the pizza arrived. The conversation eased toward other topics, with Joey occasionally name-dropping his children and their pastimes. Tracey told herself not to feel jealous when he mentioned them. After all, a man who loved his children was the best sort of man. Even Malcolm, whom she'd considered to be an outright horrible person, had revealed himself to be a doting father. People were capable of so many contradictions. Therein lay the beauty of being a human.

Tracey and Joey ate heartily. It reminded Tracey of long-ago nights when they'd downed plenty of pizza, beer, and cocktails, always with room in their bellies for more. After they finished the final slice, Joey suggested that they head to a bar, asking, "I don't suppose The Pink Pony is still open?"

Tracey gasped with laughter. "You think that old place would ever close?"

"I prayed it never would."

Joey insisted on paying. Tracey watched him hand over his credit card easily, hardly looking at the bill itself. This was a far cry from the younger Joey, who'd mostly crashed on people's couches (that is, when he hadn't stayed with Tracey, which he mostly had during the latter part of his island stay). This reminded Tracey of another pretty enormous question. *Where did Joey plan on staying while on the island? Flying drunk wasn't exactly a recommended late-night activity.*

The Pink Pony was just as vibrant as ever, with tourists out front whipping their arms as they told exciting stories, normal bar revelers seated at the bar, their heads bowed over their beers, and a trim and healthy Marcy slinging drinks, just as ever. As Tracey entered, Marcy winked at her before returning her attention to another order at the bar.

Given that it was Saturday night, Tracey was surprised to find a little table in the back, recently vacated and sticky from someone's spilled Rum Runner drink. Joey laughed and said, "Gosh, this place is just how I remember it."

Marcy hustled over with a rag and smeared it across the table. "Tracey Swartz. I haven't seen the likes of you in this establishment in quiet a while. In fact, I've seen very little of you at all— since I saw a little too much of you, if you know what I mean."

Laughter rolled over Tracey comfortably as she settled into the stool. She'd nearly forgotten that Marcy had caught Cindy and Tracey in the midst of a skinny-dipping excursion.

"Promise me that you'll tease Cindy to death about that next time you see her," Tracey said.

Joey was seated on the stool across from her. He threw his hands in the air, then said, "Feels like I'm missing something."

Marcy studied Joey, her eyebrows lurking over her eyes. After a dramatic pause, she snapped her fingers, "Joey! I would have recognized you anywhere."

Joey's jaw flew open in shock. He looked as though he'd seen a ghost.

"Wait. I know your name. Give me a sec. I got it, I got it..." He tapped the side of his head.

"I don't think your memory has anything on Marcy's," Tracey said, her heart ballooning. "I always tell her that she should enter memory competitions."

"What the heck would I do in a memory competition?" Marcy rolled her eyes. "Are you reckless kids going to order, or am I going to have to kick you out? Not that I haven't kicked both you and Joey out, at the same time, before."

"Oh. That night!" Tracey's smile nearly cracked her face. She and Joey locked eyes.

"How many Rum Runners did we have that night?" Joey asked.

"Eight? Maybe nine?"

"At least," Marcy shot out. "I take it you want a Rum Runner again for old time's sake?"

"Why the heck not, Margaret," Joey tried.

Marcy's eyes flashed. "That's not my name, you imbecile. But I see you're just as confident as ever." She then locked eyes with Tracey and added, "You take care of yourself around him."

With Marcy back at the bar stirring their Rum Runners, Joey puffed out his cheeks and said, "Well, that was ominous."

Tracey waved a hand. "Marcy just likes to remind everyone at the bar that she's the boss."

"Marcy. That's right. I knew it started with an M."

The Rum Runners went down smoothly, potentially too smoothly. The bright liquid stained their tongues and made their conversations comical. They began to discuss the "winding road of life" and soon, with the second and third Rum Runner, commenced to talking about their regrets and the lives they might have had if only things had gone a little bit differently.

"Oh, come on!" Tracey cried. "You have to be kidding me. You're a pilot, for goodness sake. And Nashville seems like such a cool town."

Joey shifted his head this way, then that, as though he wasn't entirely sure he agreed. "Grass is always greener on the other side. You know?" He pointed his thumb back toward the Straits of Mackinac. "You know this island and your friends and your family so well. You must feel the love for all of it in your very bones. I've always been such a wanderer. Reckless, maybe, but overwhelmed with searching for the next best thing."

Tracey's heart surged. *Was that why he'd left her in the first place? Was that why he was there with her that night— that he couldn't make do with the life he'd built with his wife?*

Oh, but it couldn't matter. Not right now. They were halfway through their fourth Rum Runner, and the laughter had begun to bubble wildly as they swapped stories of the times they remembered, the mistakes they'd made. If Tracey remembered correctly, he'd been a ridiculously good kisser. She'd once told Cindy that the kisses she shared with Joey reminded her of romantic films. "They just sweep you up," she'd said.

After a flurry of alcohol and laughter, Tracey and Joey suddenly stood in front of her front porch. Tracey's keys jangled at her side. *What time was it?* The moon hung low in the night sky, casting an ominous glow, as though it wanted to reprimand Tracey for bad behavior.

But she wouldn't go there. No matter how much her heart wanted it.

Once inside, she poured them both glasses of water and listened to another of Joey's stories about pilot school. When he stepped into the bathroom, she pulled the bed out from the couch and stretched clean sheets over it. She wasn't the Tracey from 1999 anymore, no matter how much she craved that version of herself. Instead, she was a Tracey with clean sheets. She was a Tracey with an early-morning shift on Monday.

"Oh." Joey eyed the bed in the living room. He pressed a hand over his heart, as though prepared to make some kind of speech. (*"Tracey, I've loved you my whole life."* Well, maybe that was all in her head.)

But after only a beat, he smiled, then said, "Thank you so much. I'm beat."

"Me too." Tracey scratched the back of her head. "You need a toothbrush, or...?"

"No. I'm good."

The air swelled between them, as though someone needed to acknowledge just how weird this actually was.

"Okay! Goodnight!" Tracey sped down the hallway and into her bedroom, where she closed the door, collapsed on the bed, and stared into space.

For the next ten minutes, she remained wide awake, too frightened and riled up to sleep. But then, in a wink, she fell into a deep sleep. She didn't wake until the sun crawled high into the morning sky.

Chapter Fifteen

The sunlight was an assault. Tracey squinted as she made her way out of her bedroom and headed for the kitchen to brew the biggest pot of coffee ever known to man. She'd forgotten about the horror of Rum Runner hangovers, and in fact, now that she staggered forward, she remembered her promise to Cindy that she would "never, ever drink a Rum Runner again." Joey Gilbert was the sort of man who made you forget all the promises you'd made to yourself.

At least she hadn't done something that she would really regret.

But when she stepped into the living room, she found that the couch had already been made-up. The sheets had been removed and folded neatly on the couch cushions. There was no sign of Joey at all.

Exhausted, Tracey collapsed on a couch cushion and studied her toes. Emma had recently painted them a horrible turquoise color. Tracey hadn't had the heart to tell her how much she detested it.

Where on earth had Joey gone? Was it possible that he'd

done that singularly adorable thing that guys in romantic comedies did— gone out to get baked goods or bagels so that they could eat together and recover from their hangovers? Tracey's heart seized with hope. For a full thirty seconds, she stared at the front door expectantly, her head pounding with her headache.

Come on, Tracey. Make yourself a dang pot of coffee. He's not coming back.

Tracey walked toward the kitchen and watched as the coffee pot sputtered up some piping hot, black liquid. This was her secret to a new lease on life. Or whatever.

Only with the mug of coffee before her could Tracey fully face the horror of what she'd just experienced. She'd stupidly created a fantasy of the "one who'd gotten away." If she was honest, she'd even had fantasies about Joey, Emma, and Tracey all getting dinner together one of these days, bantering and laughing like any good family should.

It was a Sunday. The following morning, Tracey would be needed on set by seven for a good twelve hours of difficult work. It was hard for Tracey to wrap her mind around that. She closed the curtains as tightly as she could, frightened of the sun and what it could continue to do to her already-pounding head. With the living room TV on low, she watched two hours of reality television, alternating an ice pack across her neck and her forehead.

Around two, there came the sound of a key at the front door. Tracey lifted her shoulders slightly, listening intently. Next came the soft tap-tap-tap of Emma's footfalls just before she appeared in the living room. She looked bright and carefree, her hair curlier than usual, her skin glowing.

She looked like a picture-perfect, newly pregnant woman.

"Hi, honey!" Tracey's voice rasped.

"Mom. What's up? I've been calling you."

Tracey had shoved her phone between the couch cushions.

The lack of message from Joey had irritated her. She rubbed her eyes and searched through her soul for some energy. If there was anything a mother knew how to do, it was "fake it" with her children.

"Oh, gosh. I've just had this migraine," Tracey lied.

Emma moaned. "You've been working yourself to death on set."

Tracey waved a hand. "Don't worry about it. I'll be right as rain by tomorrow."

Emma disappeared into the kitchen. She knocked about, opening and closing cabinets and the fridge. When she returned, she carried a cheese sandwich on a bright blue plate, a big glass of water, and two aspirins. She placed them gently on the coffee table, urging her mother to care for herself. In truth, if Emma hadn't been there, Tracey wasn't sure she would have bothered to eat that day.

"I'm back on set tomorrow," Emma said as she settled into the chair nearest the couch.

Tracey swallowed the pills and drank several gulps of water. "That's exciting!"

"Yeah. Megan and I both were called back to work as bartenders," Emma explained.

"I'll find the perfect costumes for both of you."

Emma's face brightened; her big blue eyes shone. So many of her facial features were tied to her father's, so much so that Tracey's heart stirred with sorrow. *How she wished her daughter could experience the magic that was Joey Gilbert. How she wished he would have just stayed.*

"How did it go last night?" Tracey asked.

"Megan said she basically already knew," Emma said with a shrug. "I guess it's impossible to live that closely with someone and hide something as big as a pregnancy."

"Ugh. Give me the 'worst mother of the year' award," Tracey countered.

"No way. We don't live together anymore. It was easier to hide it from you."

Tracey and Emma held one another's gaze for a long time. Tracey wanted to ask her daughter, yet again, why she wanted to hide such an enormous life event from her. But that question was so intricately tied up in Tracey's own secret story.

"Come on," Emma said firmly, pointing at the sandwich. "Eat up. You need your strength for the week."

Tracey's smile widened. "See? You're already nagging. That's the sign of a great mom."

"You're funny," Emma shot back, then rolled her eyes playfully.

* * *

"It's perfect, Tracey. Really." Donna stood off to the right of the changing area, her hands on her hips. Tracey made a final adjustment on Emma's barmaid uniform, pinning the top so that it hung beautifully across her collarbones. "Where did you find that dress?"

"It was in the trailer," Tracey explained. "On the rack in the back."

"Wow. You scavenged all the way back there?" Donna sounded impressed. She then eyed Emma knowingly and said, "Your mom is the real deal. I can't believe you've kept her in Michigan all these years. We could really use her out in California."

Emma laughed good-naturedly and agreed. "You should have seen some of the Halloween costumes she made me as a kid."

Donna, uninterested in things like Halloween costumes, soon found something else to attend to. Megan popped out from the changing stall in her own barmaid costume, whipping her hair over her shoulder. Back on set, one of the assistant directors howled that it was time to roll.

"Go! Go! Go!" Tracey sounded like a softball coach. She watched as Emma and Megan hustled to their position behind the bar counter, where another assistant director waited to explain exactly what they needed to do during the shoot.

In the interim, Tracey paid attention to the other extras on set, ensuring they had enough water and were well-fed (with snacks that wouldn't stain their costumes, of course). As far as she could tell, Megan and Emma did a stellar job behind the bar, chatting with the extras who stood just behind the table where the two main characters sat.

The main characters in this scene played a drinking game that involved asking each other probing questions about one another's lives, which remained a mystery for both. When they didn't want to answer the question, or it felt too intimate, they took a drink. As they got tipsier and tipsier, the secrets began to spill out of them.

Gosh. If only she and Joey had played a game like that.

Then again, they'd had enough alcohol for secret-telling—yet had avoided it. How? Why?

After several takes, Malcolm called out, "Great, everyone. Really good work. Let's take a fifteen-minute break. Grab some water. Have a snack. In the next scene, we're still in this bar, but Hank is by himself. We only need one of the bartenders, as well." Malcolm tapped his chin contemplatively, "It's Emma, right? You feel okay about sticking around?"

Emma's face brightened. Megan squeezed her upper arm excitedly. As Megan headed off to grab a bottle of water, Malcolm approached Emma. Tracey, about ten feet away, working diligently on another costume design, eavesdropped all she could.

"Hey there. Thanks for sticking around. For continuity's

sake, it's important to have one of the same bartenders around for this next scene," Malcolm explained.

"It's my pleasure!"

Malcolm's laughter was sincere. "Great. Good to hear." After a pause, he added, "Are you feeling any better?"

"A lot better. Thanks a lot for asking."

Tracey lifted her head to investigate the strange scene. When she did, she accidentally locked eyes with Malcolm. His dark eyes smoldered. *What on earth?* He then returned his attention to Emma and began to explain to her how he wanted the next scene to play out. "This scene is much more heartbreaking because Hank's love has left the island forever. He knows he's never going to see her again."

Donna shuffled up alongside Tracey. She carried about ten dresses on hangers that hung from a single, bony finger. Under her breath, she said, "I heard what Malcolm just said to your daughter. I have to say, I've never heard Malcolm exhibit such empathy before."

"I'm glad he apologized," Tracey whispered.

"Yeah. But. Come on, Tracey." Donna scoffed. "People don't apologize in Hollywood."

Tracey considered telling Donna about her interaction with Malcolm from last Saturday. But that story, in and of itself, seemed too complicated and too personal. Malcolm had a daughter, an ex-wife, and a life filled with obvious regrets. These stories had nothing to do with Donna. They had nothing to do with Tracey, either.

"By the way," Donna continued as she re-hung the clothes on a nearby iron rack. She no longer looked at Tracey. "I'm also one of those Hollywood jerks who don't apologize. And I certainly don't just give out compliments. You should take each of mine to heart. You have real skill, Tracey. Remember that."

After shooting finished later that day, Tracey and Emma

floated home, chatting excitedly about the day and Emma's "big break" as a stand-in bartender in a film.

"I'm just glad I haven't started to show!" Emma said. "The camera adds ten pounds already."

"The camera loves you. Don't you dare think anything else," Tracey said.

When they returned home, Emma slid a frozen pizza into the oven and called Megan to tell her about the rest of the shoot. Tracey poured herself a small glass of chardonnay and removed her shoes from her aching feet slowly.

"I just love that turquoise color on your toes," Emma interrupted her conversation with Megan to say.

Tracey grinned. "Me too." Maybe she was coming around to the color, after all. Or maybe she just loved Emma too much not to love turquoise nail polish, too.

As Emma chatted and the pizza crisped in the oven, Tracey's phone buzzed on the counter. She reached for it without fear, thinking it would be a message from Cindy or Elise or even Donna, still panicking about the next day's shoot.

But instead, the message was from Joey Gilbert.

JOEY: Hey. I'm sorry I had to leave Mackinac early yesterday morning.

JOEY: I had to be in Nashville by the afternoon to prepare for today's intense flight schedule. (I'm in Orlando now, if you can believe it.)

JOEY: I didn't want to wake you up. I know you needed the sleep.

JOEY: But Tracey, I loved seeing you. It was just like old times.

JOEY: And I'd love to do it all again if you'll have me.

Tracey's head pounded. She read and reread the messages, no longer fully in tune with her body or her heart. *Why did he want to see her again? Did he feel what she felt? Could she forgive him for just leaving like that, without even a note to say goodbye?* Then again, he was a pilot with a difficult schedule. She couldn't blame him for that.

Emma snapped her fingers near her face and said, "Earth to Tracey! Are you still there?"

Tracey practically threw her phone to the side, frightened that she'd forgotten that Emma was right there. "Huh? Oh. Is the pizza ready?"

"Just about." Emma frowned. "You look white as a sheet. You should really go sit down."

Come on, Tracey. Pull yourself together.

"I'm really okay." Tracey did her best to smile. It felt strained.

"If you say so," Emma said reluctantly.

As Emma turned back to grab two plates from the cabinet, Tracey grabbed her phone and spontaneously sent a text message that she would probably come to regret.

TRACEY: You're welcome any time.

"I hope you're ready for some good, old-fashioned frozen pizza!" Emma exclaimed. "Just like the good old days, when it was just the two of us."

Tracey's heart lifted at the memories. "I'm sorry I was such a bad mother. I should have made more salad."

Emma's grin was mischievous. "There's tomato in the sauce."

Chapter Sixteen

The next week and a half passed like this. Tracey awoke at five in the morning, went for a three-mile run, showered, did her hair and makeup, and rushed to the set, where she tore through twelve to thirteen hours of work alongside Donna. Often, she made up her own costumes for the scenes at-a-glance, based on whatever she found lying around the costume trailers. More than once, Donna gave her a "compliment," or her version of one, while Malcolm often caught her eye as she scampered past, making her stomach tighten in that peculiar way.

The film itself had fallen into an easy rhythm, with many people experienced in the film world saying that time was "flying by." Tracey heard more than one member of the staff say something like, "I really don't want this shoot to end. I've fallen in love with Mackinac."

Oftentimes when Tracey returned home, her mind returned to Joey, who still hadn't written since her promise that he was "welcome any time." Tracey now felt terribly foolish for having said that. Still, when these thoughts became too powerful, her exhaustion from the film set overtook them and sent her into a deep sleep.

After that, she'd wake up and perform her schedule all over again, like a machine.

Toward the end of July, Tracey hustled over to the side of the set to refill her bottle of water. It was mid-eighties and stifling hot, and her tongue felt like sandpaper. Malcolm had just allowed them a full twenty-minute break, which was largely unheard of in the film community. Donna, even, had sequestered herself off in the shade with a green smoothie and enormous sunglasses. You could see from her face that she didn't want to be disturbed.

As Tracey filled her water bottle, she made a mental list of the tasks she still needed to get done before the cameras rolled again. There were collars to fix and pants to hem. On top of that, the main actress had to try on the trench coat a final time to make sure that it actually fit her slim shoulders.

Tracey sipped the water with her eyes closed. She then stepped back to allow a woman in the lighting department to fill her bottle. As she turned back, she noticed Malcolm toward the far end of the set with his phone pressed hard against his ear.

Yet again, she could make out bits and pieces of his side of the conversation.

But this time, he sounded close to tears.

"You know that I'll pay for it. I'll pay for everything," he said. "The school is our only answer." After another pause, he said, "Don't say that. You know that I care about so much more than the money."

Tracey took a delicate step toward him. It was like he was a wounded animal in need of care.

"Please. Can you put her on video? It's been so long since I've seen her," Malcolm continued. "Did she like the dresses? Did you?"

Tracey's heart shattered. After another moment, Malcolm's voice shifted, becoming gritty and angry. If Tracey was correct and he now spoke to his ex-wife, it was clear that his ex-wife wanted only his money and nothing more.

Tracey forced herself away from Malcolm's tragedy. When she returned to her side of the set, Donna barked that at least four extras had complained that their costumes were "itchy." "I guess we need to do something about these drama queens," she said with a sigh.

As Tracey forced herself through the next steps of hemming, talking to annoying extras, and patching up holes in trousers, her head stewed with worry.

Malcolm's conversation reminded her that she still hadn't told Joey or Emma about one another. It was obviously wrong not to allow a father to see his daughter. It was so wrong that it nearly destroyed one of the strongest and bull-headed men she knew.

"Does that feel better?" Tracey asked an extra, who'd swapped out an itchy vest for a button-up.

The extra began to complain about something else. He pivoted in the mirror, inspecting the way the button-up hugged his back. Tracey could hardly hear what he said. Her mind swam with confusion.

During another break, later on, Tracey grabbed her phone and began to write a message to Joey. Why the heck shouldn't she? They were friends, weren't they? It was best not to overthink these things.

TRACEY: Hey there! How's the rest of your summer going?

It was casual. Easy. The sort of thing a "normal" friend would ask. *Right?* She shoved the phone back in her pocket and chased after an extra whose collar had a big, brown stain on it. What had he eaten since she'd last put him in that shirt? Was he trying to kill her?

"Easy, tiger," she said to him. "Let's get you changed."

Women, Tracey knew, were terribly good at making up excuses for the men they wanted to love.

Over the next several hours, Tracey made up several excuses for why Joey hadn't written her back. He was probably in the air, flying several hundreds of people from Nashville to Dallas or Memphis to Newark or Seattle to Denver. Or, he was running his children to soccer practice or ballet rehearsal, checking their math problems, or mowing the lawn. There were all sorts of reasons people couldn't text back right away.

Three days later, however, Tracey's excuses for Joey had run thin. She was grumpy and irritable about it, so much so that Emma asked if there was something wrong. Tracey told Emma that she was just exhausted from set. Perhaps this was partially true.

But late at night, as Tracey tossed and turned and ached with loneliness, she tried to come to terms with the fact that Joey was out of her life, this time for good. He'd clearly come to Mackinac for one thing and one thing only— and she hadn't given him that. She could only be happy with herself for that.

Besides, he'd already given her the greatest gift of all— Emma. What more could she possibly want?

Tracey then did the most adult thing she could possibly think to do. She grabbed her phone and blocked Joey's number, thus officially deleting the past and giving all her power and strength to the future. This was the only way forward.

Chapter Seventeen

Sunday was the final day of July and a sincerely tragic one for the Swartz family. On August 1st, Cindy and Megan would take four suitcases of Megan's belongings off the island, stuff them into a rental vehicle, and drive down to East Lansing. There, Cindy would move Megan into her brand-new apartment, located just close enough to campus for Megan to walk to class. And after that, Megan would begin her off-island life.

Despite her own optimism about her baby and her future, Emma's eyes were damp for much of the day. As she carried the beautifully decorated cake onto Cindy's back patio, several tears traced down her cheeks. She placed the cake in front of Megan and clapped her hands along with everyone else. "Good luck!" echoed across the porch and off the Straits of Mackinac.

Megan leaped into Emma's arms and hugged her as though her life depended on it. From where Tracey stood, she could just barely make out Megan's whisper, "I don't know what I'm going to do without you."

"Same," Emma said.

After cake, Tracey, Cindy, and Elise scrubbed dinner plates and cake plates in the kitchen while the rest of the Swartz family chatted on the porch. Cindy's cheeks were blotchy, and she seemed slightly withdrawn.

"You went through this with Penny and Brad," Tracey said to Elise. "Any words of wisdom."

Elise's face crumpled. "It never gets any easier. You just get used to it."

Cindy hiccupped. She then rinsed off a plate and stacked it angrily in the drying rack. Tracey held her breath. She wished she could tell Cindy about Emma's pregnancy right then. Babies were always something to look forward to. They created optimism and a new sense of life.

She also wished she could tell her about the whole drama with Joey. In truth, because Marcy had spotted Joey and Tracey at The Pink Pony, she was overwhelmingly surprised that nobody knew about it already. Marcy was ordinarily the queen of gossip— and she had buckets of it. *What had stopped her from gossiping this time?*

"Megan just keeps promising me that she'll be back in four years," Cindy said, hiccupping again. "But how can she come back to the island after knowing so much about the world?"

Elise's eyes shimmered. "I never knew anything about this island until last year. Now, I'm a full-time resident. The magic here is extraordinary. Megan won't forget that."

Before they left for the night, Tracey helped Cindy load up the cart that she and Megan would wheel down to the ferry the following morning, bright and early.

"I'm sorry I can't see you off," Tracey said sheepishly.

"You have bigger fish to fry on set," Cindy told her firmly. "And don't you forget it."

Tracey wrapped her older sister in a hug and tilted her

right, then left, her eyes clamped closed. She felt her sister's heart breaking, and she so wished the take the pain away.

Tracey knew there was no taking away anyone's pain. Cindy had to carry it, just as Tracey had to carry her own. They could only relieve the sorrow with laughter and love.

* * *

That Thursday, Donna allowed Tracey an afternoon off to take Emma to her next ultrasound. When Tracey thanked Donna profusely, Donna lifted a hand to say, "If you thank me one more time, I'll throw up. You Midwesterners and your niceties. It's too much." Tracey had a good laugh about that.

Emma and Tracey sat in the waiting room of the ultrasound clinic, which was really a three-seated lobby with a bad painting of a duck on the wall. Emma texted Megan and passed the information along to Tracey, saying, "Apparently, there's a really attractive guy who lives down the hallway from her. She says she hates it because it means she can't leave the house looking like crap."

Tracey giggled. "Tell her that once you can look like crap in front of someone, that's when it's real love."

Not that Tracey had ever allowed herself to look like crap in front of anyone. Her stomach surged with sudden fear. *Had she ever actually been in love?*

On cue, the ultrasound technician called them into the little room. She greeted Emma warmly, as this was already her second time at the clinic itself.

"I see you brought someone along with you this time," the tech said as she prepared the lubricant to go over Emma's abdomen.

"She was scolding me last time for having not told anyone," Emma explained to Tracey. Her words were light and airy, such a contrast to how frightened she must have been last time. Probably, the tech had seen just how terrified she'd been.

With the ultrasound gel spread across Emma's stomach, the tech pressed the probe over the gel and flashed an image up on the black-and-white screen. Tracey watched the screen with bated breath, suddenly terrified. A thousand thoughts of "what could go wrong in pregnancy" flooded her mind.

But a split-second later, the technician whispered, "Wow. Look at that."

Tracey and Emma were wide-eyed, watching as a tiny, tiny baby appeared— nothing more than a head, the whisper of some arms, some legs, and a little belly. It was the most beautiful thing Tracey had seen since her own ultrasound before Emma's birth. Laughter bubbled through her as she squeezed Emma's hand.

"Look at that!" Tracey squealed.

Emma's eyes were heavy with tears. "Does the baby look healthy?"

The technician studied the black-and-white screen. "Everything looks good, Emma. Really good." She paused and then asked, "Do you want to hear the heartbeat again this time?"

The answer was obvious. With headphones on, first Emma listened to the steady thump-thump of her baby's heartbeat; afterward, Tracey took over. Her eyes closed, as she allowed herself to fall into the steady undertow of this human's first few beats. She prayed for millions and millions of more beats. She prayed for this baby's healthy and beautiful life.

* * *

"I don't know. A boy could be good," Emma said, stirring her green smoothie and wearing a pained expression. "But a girl? I mean, all those little frilly outfits. And those dresses you always have at the boutique! Can you imagine the kinds of things we could find for her?"

Tracey laughed and sipped her own green smoothie, a concoction of spinach and raspberries and other vitamins, which Emma and Tracey had decided to call their substitute for Friday afternoon wine.

"Why are you laughing?" Emma asked.

"I just remember having these same thoughts when I was pregnant with you. But when you came out into the world, I realized that it was always you the whole time. That wondering about boy versus girl or which name to call you was almost a waste of time. You were so uniquely you from the moment I met you," Tracey said.

Emma tightened her cheeks. "Don't mess with me like that right now, Mom. You know that the hormones make me cry almost constantly. I'd like to go just one hour without sobbing."

Tracey's throat tightened. She, too, had cried quite often recently— for a variety of reasons. Without the possibility of Joey texting her back, she felt withdrawals. The emotion he'd brought into her life had felt like a storm. That, on top of the baby, Megan's departure, and the sheer onslaught of the film, had made her very emotional.

"By the way," Emma began tentatively. "With Megan gone, that apartment over the fudge shop is feeling really big."

Tracey burned with sudden hope. "I can imagine."

"I was thinking about giving it up. The owner says his niece and her husband want the place, anyway."

"I see." Tracey sipped more of her smoothie. "You know that you're welcome here."

Emma's cheeks became pink with embarrassment. "It's just that, well..."

"It'll be hard work, Em," Tracey told her. "The hardest work of your life. The only way I got through it was because your Grandma Mandy helped me every step of the way."

Emma nodded, locking eyes with Tracey. She'd made her point.

"But don't rush yourself," Tracey told her. "You're only three and a half months along. Your room will be here when you need it. And we can turn the office into a nursery easily. In fact, I don't know why we even have that little office. We hardly use it."

"It is dusty in there," Emma agreed, her smile widening.

It was settled. Tracey's heart ballooned with the promise of this new era, during which she could throw herself totally into her role as a grandmother. She would be Emma's rock, the way Mandy had been for her. And the Swartz family line would go on, from one strong woman to another.

Around seven-thirty that evening, Tracey suggested that they order delivery and stay in for the night. Although they were still on the porch, the idea of walking downtown for a brief grocery run or a restaurant take-out order sounded borderline exhausting. Emma agreed wholeheartedly.

"When the little one is here, we'll cook plenty of healthy meals," Tracey affirmed as she grabbed her phone to dial their favorite Chinese place.

"Yeah! Plenty."

"Fruits. Vegetables. Protein sources. You, me, and baby will be just about as healthy as can be," Tracey continued as she typed the number, which she'd memorized for the better part of twenty years.

"Ugh. I'm on hold," Tracey announced as a horrible jingle began to play from her phone's speaker.

"Hasn't Jeff gotten the hint that we hate that jingle?" Emma asked.

"I think he does it to torture his customers," Tracey said.

"It's working," Emma affirmed.

As the jingle continued to boop and beep on the other line, Tracey watched a lazy bird swoop across the gorgeous orange and yellow sky. Her heart ached with summertime nostalgia. Very soon, autumn would wreak havoc across the island and latch them inside.

"Come on..." Tracey moaned into the receiver. Emma laughed that gorgeous laugh of hers.

Suddenly, a man in a black t-shirt and a black baseball hat leaped from the shadows of the main road and half-stumbled, half-stomped up the walkway. Tracey jumped from her chair, frightened of how violently he raced toward the house.

It took her more than a few seconds to realize that the man who stormed them was Joey Gilbert. She immediately dropped the phone. The jingle didn't quit, however, and still booped and beeped through the air, sounding terribly sinister.

"Dammit, Tracey!" Joey howled from the walkway. He sounded borderline insane.

"What are you doing here?" Tracey demanded.

Joey's eyes were heavy with tears. He looked up at Tracey as though she was the only woman he'd ever known.

"I flew here this morning, Tracey. I couldn't take it. Why are you ignoring me? We have something special, Tracey. Please." Joey placed his palms together and stared up at her.

Tracey's heart twitched. For the first time in a long time, she was utterly speechless.

"Listen to what your heart tells you, Tracey," Joey whispered. He wavered slightly on his feet. For the first time, Tracey understood that he was terribly intoxicated.

"Where have you been since you landed?" Tracey demanded.

Joey waved a hand back behind him. "The Pink Pony. Other bars. Mackinac Island has always had its fair share of, shall we say, resources."

Very, very slowly, Emma turned her head to face her mother. Her expression looked tortured. "Mom. Who is this?" she rasped.

At this, Joey threw his head back so that his laughter echoed out across the island. Both Emma and Tracey watched him, petrified.

Finally, Joey spoke. The way he said it made the truth exceedingly obvious.

"Who do you think I am, honey?"

Chapter Eighteen

Immediately after Joey's surprise (and wholly unwelcome) arrival, he nearly collapsed. Tracey leaped to catch him and then struggled to drag his drunk form up the porch steps, through the foyer and living room, then all the way to the dark shadows of her bedroom. There, she placed him gently beneath her comforter and listened to the sounds of his snores. She wanted to smack him and say, *"Do you know what you've done?"* But what good would that do? He was a terribly unhappy man who'd created a terribly unhappy situation.

As she tip-toed back to the dying light on the front porch, Emma's voice carried through the crack in the door.

"Buckle up, Jeff, because I have a big order for you. Crab Rangoons. Egg Rolls. Sweet and Sour Chicken and Sesame Chicken. Oh, maybe more Egg Rolls. Something beefy. What do you recommend?"

Tracey waited for Emma to finish out her larger-than-life Chinese order before she opened the door a little wider and leaned against the doorframe. Emma sat with her feet propped up on the opposite chair. The orange sunset glowed across her cheeks and forehead, illuminating her gorgeous hair. What Tracey could make out of Emma's expression told her that she was woefully confused.

"Honey..." Tracey began.

But to this, Emma just shook her head. "Not until I've eaten."

Apparently, Jeff at the Chinese place sensed Emma's urgency. He had the food finished and delivered in twenty-five minutes flat. Tracey arranged the boxes of fried rice and fried snacks and sauce-heavy meats across the patio table, her heart pounding. Emma clicked her chopped sticks together and surveyed the feast.

They ate what they could, both wordless. It was almost like an out-of-body experience, especially for a mother-daughter duo who so often couldn't shut up around one another. With Joey sleeping off his drunkenness in the next room, their tongues were stumped.

Would Emma finding out about this destroy Tracey and Emma's relationship forever? Would Emma decide not to move in? Worse— would Emma choose to move to East Lansing to have her baby closer to Megan? Tracey's mind raced with thousands of possibilities, none of them fully logical and all of them heartbreaking.

After about a half-hour of sweet and salty chicken, gooey Crab Rangoons, delicious fried rice, and whatever else they could wrap their chopsticks around, Emma placed her chopsticks along her plate, crossed her arms over her chest, and took full stock of her mother. Tracey knew the stoic expression on Emma's face well. It always meant business.

"This is quite a way to find out," Emma said suddenly. Her voice simmered with sarcasm.

Tracey's throat tightened. "I never would have planned it like this."

"How would you have planned it?"

Tracey swallowed several times. Emma's eyes were so intense; it was like staring at the sun. "It's such a long story, Emma."

"We have nothing but time."

"Okay. You're right." She grimaced. "I met him on the island twenty-three years ago. He was a vagabond. A sailor. When I found out I was pregnant, he was long gone."

"That guy?" Emma pointed back toward the house.

"I thought I'd never see him again. He was never in our lives, and that was fine with me. But a little more than a month ago, we saw each other at the Los Angeles airport. It was like seeing a ghost."

Emma's lips parted in surprise.

"Neither of us said anything. But a few days later, he wrote me, asking if that really had been me. We started texting, catching up and telling one another about our lives. It felt really good to have his voice in my head again. I felt young and carefree and alive.

"A few weeks ago, he visited the island. I'm not sure what he was looking for when he came here. We talked for hours. I could feel myself wanting to fall in love with him all over again. But it's impossible. Life has taken us in two different directions. I eventually decided to block him on everything so that he couldn't contact me anymore. It was too intense."

Emma puffed out her cheeks. "Cue him storming our front porch, demanding why you're ignoring him."

"Exactly." Tracey wiped a tear from her cheek. "I'm so sorry I didn't tell you about this, Emma. I always wanted to. But I never thought Joey was the father type."

Emma dropped her gaze to her thighs. For a long time, the silence shivered around them.

"I've been thinking so much about him, or my idea of him, over the past six weeks," Emma whispered. "Especially now that I haven't told Grant about this baby yet."

Tracey's voice broke. "I would have told Joey if I could have. He was completely unreachable. And, if there's anything I've learned from getting to know him, it's this. He is a good father. He stepped up to the plate with his younger children. Gosh, it makes me regret that he wasn't around for you. We could have been..."

Here, Tracey trailed off, recognizing she'd gone too far. Emma's eyes bugged out.

"His younger children? You mean I have half-siblings?"

Tracey nodded. "I was going to tell you. I was going to find a way to tell you, at least."

Emma looked at her as though she didn't fully believe her. Tracey wasn't sure if she believed herself.

"I was just so overwhelmed with it all," Tracey continued to explain, praying it was enough. "I made up this whole reality in my head, where he moved to the island and became a father to you and a grandfather to your baby. It sounds insane! And it is. But I suppose I'm just a desperate mid-aged woman grasping at straws. I'm allowed those kinds of fantasies."

"Mom..." Emma stood, then walked around the table to hug her mother. She placed her head tenderly on the top of Tracey's back and heaved a sigh. "He's married, isn't he?"

Tracey nodded and inhaled sharply. She wanted to tell her daughter that Joey and his wife were on the rocks. *But was that even true?*

Bit by bit, Tracey and Emma boxed up the Chinese food leftovers, tossed out what they could, and brought the plates inside. Once there, Tracey poured herself an above-average glass of chardonnay and took a large gulp. Emma laughed the first laugh of the hour and said, "I'm with you in spirit."

Tracey pulled out the bed from the living room couch and, for the second time that summer, dressed it in freshly washed sheets. She and Emma sat propped up on pillows and turned on the television, where *Sweet Home, Alabama* played from halfway through.

"Joey storming up to your front porch like that has real romantic comedy vibes," Emma said as she nibbled at the edge of a bite-sized candy bar.

"Yeah. Or stalker vibes," Tracey quipped.

Emma laughed. "He's probably just coming to terms with this story, same as me."

"And me," Tracey added.

"Well. To be fair, you were the one who held all the cards this whole time," Emma pointed out.

"Being a single mother doesn't necessarily mean that you're holding any cards," Tracey told her. "Besides, when I first held you in my arms, I knew that Joey didn't matter at all." After a short pause, she added, "But if he's really hungover tomorrow, try not to tell him how little he matters. I don't want to make him feel any worse."

Emma giggled and burrowed herself deeper into the pillow. Tracey eyed the darkness of the hallway that led back to her bedroom.

"Do you want to see a picture of us from back then?" Tracey asked suddenly.

Emma's eyes widened. "More than anything!"

The fourth shelf on the bookcase was heavy with Emma-centric photo albums. Toward the far end of that shelf, however, Tracey had made space for her own non-mother memories. There was one album in particular that had a whole series of photographs of "Emma and Joey" before Joey had fled the island in pursuit of his vagabond lifestyle.

"Wow. Look at him. And look at you!" Emma held the outer edge of a yellowing photograph and took full stock of her mother and father. In the photograph, Joey was shirtless, and Tracey wore a yellow bikini. Her stomach was flat, and her legs were tan and muscular from long runs around the island. They held one another with one arm and domestic beer cans in their free hands. They looked like the perfect portrait of summertime.

"I really loved him," Tracey breathed.

"He is handsome," Emma affirmed. "And those eyes."

"They're your eyes, too," Tracey said softly.

Emma held the silence for a long time, flipping through the photographs and analyzing her parents' long-lost smiles. Probably, she, too, began to mourn the life she hadn't been allowed to live. It was only natural to have those feelings.

When Emma drifted off to sleep, Tracey was grateful to slip the photo album back onto the bookshelf, where it would surely remain untouched for the next three to ten years. Some things were better left in the past.

And some people were far more like ghosts than anything.

As she cozied next to her daughter, she prayed that it wouldn't be so difficult to kick their current ghost from the house. She needed him to leave so they could keep going on their journey without him.

Chapter Nineteen

There came a sudden crash and clatter from the next room. Tracey's eyes popped open. She inhaled the thick August air as something sizzled and popped. *What was going on?*

Beside her, Emma's eyes fluttered open. She stretched her arms up and over the top of the couch.

"Hello?" Tracey called, sounding both irritated and groggy.

A split second later, Joey leaped into the doorway between the kitchen and the living room. He flailed a spatula around, looking just as animated as ever. "Hey! Did I wake you?"

"Um." Tracey wanted to suggest that the noises he'd made would have woken the dead, but she kept that to herself. "What are you doing?"

Joey weaved his fingers through his thick hair. He looked embarrassed and youthful. "I woke up with the kind of guilt that could kill a man. I thought to myself, how best to ask for forgiveness from the two women I care about the most?"

Tracey couldn't help it. A small smile wiggled from one ear

to the other. He was endlessly charming. He could get away with anything. Maybe, so early in the morning, they would let him.

Tracey stepped out of bed. Her knees creaked beneath her, betraying her. She then followed after Joey into the kitchen, where he'd already stirred up a bowl of pancake batter, cracked several eggs into a skillet, and begun to sizzle and brown big, thick slabs of bacon.

"I ran out to the market this morning right when it opened," Joey explained. "I saw Marcy out on a run. The woman can move as quickly as a cheetah. At first, I didn't think she noticed me. Then, she glared at me and said, 'You again,' before speeding on by."

Tracey grabbed herself a glass and filled it with water. She laughed. "The government should really hire her for their spy department."

Joey used the spatula to flip each of the slabs of bacon easily. He then scraped at the bottom of the eggs and splayed them across a large blue plate. It was clear that he'd done this before. Tracey tried not to imagine him cooking breakfast for his "real family." Where did they think he was, this early on a Friday?

Emma appeared, rubbing her eyes. Joey greeted her more timidly, keeping a wide berth from the woman who'd once been his little girl. For a brief second, Tracey thought Joey would give Emma a full-fledged apology, but instead, he just reached for the filled pot of coffee and poured her a mug. Emma accepted it, thanking him. She didn't drink it.

"Thank you for letting me crash last night," he said easily, pouring the pancake batter into another, wider skillet. The batter was polka-dotted with fresh blueberries. "Flying across the country wears me out, but it's nice to feel I have these little safe havens here and there."

"What a free spirit," Emma suggested, not entirely unkindly.

Joey laughed. "I don't know if I have the time or the energy to be free-spirited anymore. That's the Joey your mother knew back in the day. I was a real live wire." He winked at Tracey.

"I know the type," Emma returned with a wide grin.

Joey pointed his spatula toward her, wagging his eyebrows. "Do you need me to put them in their place? I know just what to say."

Emma giggled. "I can take care of myself."

"That doesn't surprise me," Joey replied, his smile electric. "But everyone needs a helping hand, now and again."

They sat at the kitchen table, the three of them. Joey portioned out two eggs and slices of bacon for each of them. A big stack of blueberry pancakes sat in the middle, about three times too tall. Tracey watched her clock phone, which told her that she had to leave for work in about thirty minutes. She could already feel Donna's anxiety from several streets away.

"I got the good stuff," Joey explained, lifting a container of maple syrup from a tote bag. "It'll change pancakes for you forever." He pressed it into Emma's hands and slid a large pancake onto her plate, all in a single, fluid motion.

Emma blinked at the maple syrup and at the fat, fluffy pancake.

"I promise, it won't bite you," Joey explained.

Emma laughed, shrugged, and poured out several dollops of maple syrup onto the pancake. She took a slow bite and chewed. Joey watched her with rapt attention.

"So?" he asked.

Emma shook her head. "Pretty good."

"Pretty good?" Joey's voice lifted. "That's all you're going to give me?"

Emma's smile widened. "All right! All right! They're amazing! Is that what you want?"

"Damn right, that's what I want," Joey shot back, pounding his fist against the table. "I want my daughter to think of me as the best pancake maker in all the world."

"All the world? Not so sure about that. On the island of Mackinac, maybe," Emma teased.

Joey shrugged. "I'll take it. For now."

Emma chewed, her eyes glowing with captivation. Tracey wanted to snap her fingers in front of Emma's face as a way to remind her that Joey was a whole lot of colors of "problematic."

"You make these for your children. Don't you?" Emma asked suddenly.

Tracey's eyes widened in shock.

But to her surprise, Joey hardly skipped a beat. "I do," he replied simply. "They love them with sprinkles and M&Ms, but their mother isn't so keen when I over-sugar them before noon."

Emma laughed, her shoulders shaking. "But you can over-sugar me and Mom before noon all you like?"

"I figure we can start the day with a heavy breakfast, grab a hearty lunch, nab some ice cream around three, and finish out the day with pizza," Joey continued. "Because if there's anything I believe in, it's that food brings people together. And the three of us have a whole lot of catching up to do."

Emma's cheeks flushed pink. She tore her fork nervously through one of her eggs so that the yellow yolk sponged over the outer edge of her pancake.

"I have to work," Tracey interrupted the silence. She eyed Emma, trying to translate to her that she didn't have to do anything she didn't want to. They could tell Joey to get out of their house after breakfast— to go back to his family, back where he came from.

"Ah. That's too bad," Joey said. "Movie magic stops for no one, I guess." He then shifted his eyes toward Emma, who continued to chew on a gummy piece of egg white. "What about you? Want to hang out for the day? Show your old man around?"

Tracey's stomach twisted. *Wasn't this exactly what she'd wanted? Wasn't this picture-perfect breakfast, followed by a daddy-daughter hang, precisely what she'd dreamed of?* Finally, Joey would know his daughter. Finally, Emma would know her father. It wasn't up to Tracey whether or not they had a relationship.

Emma lifted her left shoulder. Her eyes echoed out her need for this. This was the first time in her life that her father had actually shown up for her. Why wouldn't she say yes to his offer?

"I'd like that," she said, sounding more confident about it than she probably felt.

Joey rubbed his palms together. There wasn't even a hint of a hangover in his face or his mannerisms.

"It's going to be a banner day," Joey said.

Tracey took another bite of pancake and tried to shove her worries aside. *This was largely a good thing, wasn't it? It had to be.*

Chapter Twenty

Tracey pressed ten pins between her lips and approached a line of ten extras, all of whom wore costumes that needed some kind of last-minute fix. Toward the far end of the set, Donna barked at the main actress that she was "sweating too much and ruining her outfit." Overhead, an August sunlight demanded their attention. It was one of the longest and most difficult days on set thus far— and it was only one-thirty in the afternoon. They had a long way to go.

"Hold this," Tracey instructed the first extra, whose pant legs hung too low over his seventies-style shoes.

"Don't stab me with the pin!" The extra looked terrified. "Donna did that last time."

"Don't worry. I'm a mother," Tracey explained as she slid the pins through the fabric with easy precision and not a drop of blood. She then waved the extra to the side and nabbed the next one. Near the head camera, one of the assistant directors had begun to howl that they were "fifteen minutes behind schedule" for the day. Malcolm looked somewhere between panicked and bored.

At the tail-end of Tracey's line of extras, Donna bobbed up, sucking her cheeks into her mouth. "I don't know if we'll make it work," she said, clearly stricken.

"We have to," Tracey told her simply. "There's no other way."

The extras were positioned across the set. The main actress and main actor appeared toward the back of the set and were instructed to walk side-by-side toward their "mark." Already, the beginnings of a sweat stain appeared on the actress's armpits.

"If we don't get this take quickly, she'll look like a sweaty athlete on screen," Donna muttered.

Malcolm worked diligently. He liked the first take, detested the second, and then took another three or four takes before instructing the actors and actresses to move on. Tracey and Donna sprung into action for another round of fixing, de-sweating, and changing the extras into other costumes. At some point, Tracey managed to drink some water, laugh with another co-worker, and accidentally lock eyes with Malcolm, who saluted her in an almost friendly fashion before turning back to the camera.

Tracey was grateful for the frantic day on set. Every time she had a brief moment to think, her head throbbed with worry for her daughter. *Was Joey trustworthy? What did Tracey actually know about him?*

"Hey! Earth to Tracey?" Donna snapped her fingers in front of Tracey's face and forced her back to reality.

Tracey considered explaining her fears to Donna but soon thought better of it. It wasn't that Donna didn't care about Tracey— she did. There just wasn't time to care about anything other than the twenty-five extras on set and the last-minute needs of each assistant director and, above all, Malcolm. They were overworked.

"Nice work, everyone!" An assistant director smacked his palms together between new set-ups and explained, "We're now only five minutes behind schedule if you can believe it! But don't pause to give yourself a pat on the back. Keep going!"

Tracey raced off to the costume trailer to grab a basket of hair accessories, which they required for the next scene. In this particular scene, the main actress gossiped with a friend outside of a coffee shop. Just now, the set decorator gave the fake coffee shop exterior a last-minute finish, adjusting the tables and displaying little flower arrangements. The set decorator's intern, a twenty-something girl, named Audrey, bickered with him about the flowers he'd decided on. "Peonies are so ugly."

The big box of hair accessories sat on the highest shelf in the costume trailer. Tracey lifted up on her tiptoes to grab it, but soon teetered back too far and accidentally tossed the big box of accessories across the floor. She cursed herself and fell to the floor, scrambling to pick every last bobby pin and hair scrunchie and barrette from the ground. Her panicked motions sent her phone flying from her pocket. It smacked the ground like a threat.

"Shoot," Tracey mumbled, grabbing her phone, and inspecting the screen. Luckily, it hadn't cracked.

But with the screen lit up, Tracey saw words that stopped her in her tracks.

12 MISSED CALLS FROM EMMA

"Oh my God," Tracey said aloud. Her voice echoed through the trailer. She leaped to her feet, making the trailer shake around her. The accessories remained strewn across the floor.

Back on set, the assistant director called that they had only ten more minutes till they needed to roll again. Tracey knew that meant she had about eight minutes to finalize the hair accessories of both the main actress and the other women on-screen. Donna was probably freaked out, wondering where Tracey had ended up.

But none of that mattered. Not with twelve missed calls from Emma.

Tracey's hand shook as the calls rang out across the island. The phone rang three times before Emma finally answered. When she did, her voice was mostly a scream.

"MOM!"

Tracey's heart shattered. "Emma? Emma, what's going on?"

Emma let out a sob. Behind that noise came another voice, a masculine one. It was Joey. Tracey couldn't make out anything he said, but he sounded frightened.

"Emma?" Tracey demanded. She sounded as angry as the assistant director.

But Emma couldn't find a way to form words. Her sobs grew louder and deeper. Tracey felt utterly helpless. She stomped her foot over a barrette and cracked it.

"Emma!" Tracey tried it a final time. "Just tell me where you are, and I'll come find you."

But suddenly, Joey was on the line. Tracey imagined smacking him so hard that her fingers formed white lines on his cheek. Obviously, this was all his fault.

"Tracey?"

"Joey, I swear to God..."

"Tracey, I have to land the plane."

Tracey lost all the feeling in her feet. Somewhere on set, the assistant director had begun to yell at someone, a poor soul who hadn't performed his duties quickly enough. Tracey could not believe this was her reality.

"You're in the plane? With my daughter?" Tracey sounded so cold.

"We're somewhere over the Upper Peninsula," Joey informed her. "Not far up, which is why the phone still works."

Were the words "not far up" supposed to ease Tracey's mind? She blinked into the shadows of the trailer, remembering the terror she'd felt on the plane to Los Angeles. *How could she save her daughter?*

"Why the hell did you take her on your plane?" Tracey demanded.

"I need to land the plane," he told her. In the background, Emma continued to howl. "We need to find a hospital. Right now."

Tracey fell to her knees. Several more hair accessories broke beneath her. "Joey. Wait. Please. Explain—"

"We're landing at Sawyer International Airport," he barked.

He then hung up the phone.

Tracey couldn't get enough air in her lungs. She inhaled, exhaled quickly and redialed Emma's number. But this time, the phone continued to ring without any answer. She imagined Joey speeding toward a very small runway. She imagined him panicking and taking the airplane off course. She imagined terrible, horrible things— and soon burst into tears of anger and fear.

She knew so little of what was going on. It was like someone had entered her life and re-written the rules of the world.

"Tracey? What the heck?" Donna's voice rang out angrily from behind her. Tracey felt rigid and unable to turn back to see her. "Tracey?" Before Tracey knew it, Donna appeared beside her, her hand on her upper back. Her eyes were fearful and angry, all at once. This was an expression all mothers knew well.

Tracey gaped at Donna. *How could she explain this?*

"Let's get you up," Donna said coaxingly. She then turned

her head quickly and called out, "We need some water over here! Right now!"

Donna and Tracey limped out of the trailer. An extra came running with a big bottle of water, which Tracey cupped with two hands like a child. Several other people on set gaped at her. It probably looked like she was losing her mind. She let out several sobs.

"We need to set up!" One of the assistant directors noticed the distraction and demanded everyone else ignore it. "Get her off set! Now!"

Tracey turned, prepared to walk away. But before she could take her second step, a large hand wrapped around her upper arm. The hand was firm and powerful. It stopped her in her tracks.

"Tracey?" Malcolm's voice was a welcome relief in her ear. "Tracey, what's going on?"

Tracey turned her head slowly. Her eyes found his impossibly dark ones. This was the man who'd bought too many tiny dresses for his daughter because he missed her too much to choose just one.

"I have to get to the Upper Peninsula," she told him point blank.

Malcolm gestured in the direction of the ferry docks. "You can leave. Take the next ferry."

But Tracey just shook her head. "There isn't enough time. They're in a plane. They're landing at Sawyer International."

Malcolm's face reflected back a small amount of the urgency Tracey now felt. After a strange, tense moment of silence, he whipped his arm back and called out, "We're done for the day."

Tracey's jaw dropped. All three of the assistant directors looked on the verge of a heart attack.

"Malcolm, we can't just stop for the day," one of them

hissed, hustling up beside him to gesture at something on his clipboard. "We'll be so behind schedule if we—"

But Malcolm's eyes bugged out of his head. He looked capable of anything. After a long pause, he returned his gaze back to Tracey. "My private plane is up at the airport. We'll go there now."

Tracey nodded, at a loss for words. As the film crew scrambled around, closing up for the day, Malcolm grabbed her hand and led her toward a nearby golf cart, which he and the assistant directors often used at various film sets to get around. Tracey sat next to him, cupping her knees as he whizzed them forward.

As Malcolm drove the cart, he called the Mackinac Airport to ask that they prepare his airplane. Tracey could hear both sides of the conversation and felt genuinely surprised that all this chaos was for her.

When the airport came into view, Tracey told him, "I'm terrified of flying."

To this, Malcolm replied, "I used to be until I learned to fly the plane myself."

Chapter Twenty-One

Being a big-time movie director allowed Malcolm to own a plane. It was a Lancair 320, just a tiny two-seater, nothing fancy. He told Tracey he liked to take it out for weekend trips to "see Michigan from above." Tracey buckled herself into the passenger seat and watched as his strong, capable hands turned the key. Her legs shook so hard that her knees banged together.

"Do you mind if I close my eyes?" Tracey asked, her words hardly a whisper.

"You can do whatever you want," Malcolm told her. "But if I were you, I'd watch. The lake looks so gorgeous from above. It's a rare treat."

Tracey bit down on her tongue, wrapped her hands tightly around her seatbelt, and forced herself to gaze down at the island as it moved away from them. Before long, the island seemed like nothing more than a mossy dot on the lake. It was remarkable that everything in her life existed there.

It was remarkable, too, that the beauty of seeing it from a distance had almost completely removed her fear. Almost.

At a safe distance above the ground, the plane seemed no longer affected by bumps of sudden air. Tracey continued to cup her knees, as though she could hold onto herself and keep herself intact. Beside her, Malcolm looked as cool as a cucumber. Probably, being a director of a major motion picture was a whole lot more stressful than flying a plane.

"Where are we going after we land at Sawyer?" Malcolm asked after a little while.

"The closest hospital," Tracey explained, her voice breaking. "I guess up in Marquette."

Malcolm held the silence. Clouds spit down beneath them, blurring together.

"It's my daughter," Tracey explained. "She's pregnant. All I can think is that something went wrong with the pregnancy."

There it was, the terrible truth that she'd wanted to ignore.

"What is she doing in Marquette?"

Tracey exhaled all the air from her lungs. "Her father came back into our lives. He's a pilot. I guess they must have taken his plane out."

"I see."

"I don't know if he knows she's pregnant," Tracey continued. "She's about three and a half months along. Healthy pregnancy so far, but..."

"But things happen," Malcolm finished the sentence for her.

Tracey couldn't bring herself to agree with him. She didn't want to live in a world where "things happened." "Things" were necessarily bad.

The flight to Sawyer International wasn't long, no more than thirty minutes. Unlike taking off, Tracey kept her eyes closed throughout the entire landing. The wheels kissed the landing strip easily, and the plane skidded to a halt before Malcolm drove it over to where they "parked" the planes. When Tracey hustled down the ladder and placed her feet on solid ground, she thanked the heavens above. She also eyed the other planes that had been parked, trying to figure out if one of them was actually Joey's. Unfortunately, she couldn't remember what his plane looked like.

Inside, Malcolm greeted one of the airport managers and asked about a "small plane" that had just come in from Mackinac.

"A young woman was on board. She had to go to the hospital," Tracey interjected, too impatient not to.

The airport manager adjusted his tie. "One of my employees drove them up to Marquette. They didn't tell us what was wrong. Just that they needed a hospital, ASAP."

"You don't have another employee willing to drive us up, do you?" Malcolm asked.

The manager loosened his tie nearly all the way. He glanced around to his other colleagues. "I could take you. We don't need that many people on the clock here."

"That would be great," Malcolm affirmed.

Malcolm had the kind of voice that just made people want to listen to him. Tracey wondered abstractly if this was a voice he'd been born with or if this voice had come with the territory of directing his feature films. Either way, it seemed incredible that they now walked behind this airport manager, who led them to a minivan that was filled with plush children's toys. At first, Tracey was grateful that they'd found a parent, someone who understood. Very soon after, however, the manager explained that the toys were for his dog, Baxter.

"He's my life," the manager said as they raced toward Marquette Hospital. "I wish I could find a job that I could bring him to. He loves being in the air, though."

Frequently throughout the drive to the Marquette Hospital, Tracey asked herself why Malcolm was still there. He could have flown back to Mackinac. He could have remained at the airport. But instead, he sat in the passenger seat of the airport manager's minivan and asked him question after question about his dog. This allowed Tracey to calm down, if only slightly. It was so boring to hear about the little personalities of someone else's pets. Boring felt good right then.

The manager drove them to the drop-off point at the emergency room. Malcolm tried to hand him a fifty-dollar bill, but the manager waved it away. "We don't do kind deeds for cash around here," he explained.

Tracey tried to memorize the manager's face if only so she could call it up later on and remember a man who'd helped during one of her darkest moments. But as she shuffled into the hospital, she was overwhelmed with other images that stamped it out. The white walls and floor of the hospital drowned her in light. A man with a broken arm scowled at her from his seat in the corner. Babies sobbed; children lay on the floor, waiting for something to happen.

Malcolm and Tracey rushed to the front desk. The woman seated there wore nurse scrubs and tried to hand Tracey a clipboard to fill out her information.

"My daughter just came here," Tracey rasped. "Her name is Emma Swartz. She's pregnant."

The woman didn't have to look it up on the computer. The hospital was too small for anything like that.

"The doctor is with her now," she explained. "Please, take a seat. I'll let you know when you can go back to see her."

Tracey breathed a small sigh of relief. Had things been worse, the nurse wouldn't have said there would be a future time that they could see one another.

"And the man who brought her in?" Tracey asked. "Where is he?"

The nurse turned her eyes from one area of the waiting room to the other. "He was just here. I'm sure he just went to get a cup of coffee or something."

She pointed toward a doorway that led down a long, skinny

hallway. Tracey raced down the corridor, hunting for Joey. Malcolm was hot on her heels. Probably, he was amazed at how much speed she had, given her age.

When Tracey turned the corner, she discovered Joey. He stood with a hand leaned against the automatic coffee machine, staring down as his Styrofoam cup as it filled with black liquid. Tracey quivered with rage, but when she finally spoke, her voice wasn't angry. It was frightened, like a little girl's.

"Joey?"

He turned around, his eyes wide. Tracey lengthened her stride and reached the coffee machine two seconds later. She had the urge to slap him but contained herself.

"Hi," he said. He placed his hands on his hips and then hung them at his side. He was so unlike the confident, swaggering guy who'd made them pancakes that morning.

"What the hell happened?" There it was. The anger she'd wanted to show him.

He shook his head, despondent. "She asked me to take her up. She couldn't believe I was a pilot. I wanted to show off for her, you know. But we hit a patch of turbulence. It wasn't anything major. Suddenly, she looked really pale and didn't talk for a little while. I thought she was just a little bit afraid and that the fear would eventually go away. But then, she ran to the back of the plane. Back there, she screamed. I was so frightened that I thought I would lose control of the plane."

Tracey clamped her hand over her mouth. She thought she would throw up. A steady hand appeared at her shoulder, holding her upright. It was Malcolm's.

"She hustled up and sobbed. She started trying to call you, but the calls weren't going through. She demanded we land the plane. Finally, she started getting through to you, but you weren't answering. That's when she broke down and told me that she was pregnant and bleeding terribly," he continued.

"What!?"

"Jesus," Malcolm whispered.

"When you called, that was the height of the chaos. We were closing in on the airstrip. I was so scared that I would land badly and make everything worse," he confessed. "But the landing was okay. More than okay, actually. And we took off for the hospital as soon as possible. The guy who drove us broke all land records. I can tell you that."

Tracey didn't know how to respond to that. She wasn't so keen on reckless driving with her pregnant daughter in the vehicle.

"They took her back a little while ago and haven't told me anything," he said. "I'm surprised you got here so quickly."

Tracey's throat was tight. She inhaled all the air she could, but it still wasn't enough. Malcolm and Joey had a conversation that she couldn't fully understand. At some point, she heard Malcolm say, "I have a plane on the island." Joey gave him a nod of recognition. Pilots.

There was a long pause. Joey took his Styrofoam cup, drank it, and wrinkled his nose.

"Why didn't you tell me she was pregnant?" Joey finally asked.

Tracey shook her head. She hadn't even told him about Emma at all. *Why would she have told him this intimate detail?*

Malcolm's hand remained on Tracey's shoulder. After a long, terrible pause, he said, "I'm going to get us some water from the cafeteria."

The thought of staying with Joey, alone in the hallway, filled Tracey with dread. She locked eyes with Malcolm and heard herself say, "I'm coming with you." Malcolm nodded and laced his fingers through hers, guiding her back toward the cafeteria and out of sight of Joey.

As they waited in line for water, Malcolm sniffed. "That guy is a piece of work."

Tracey knew he was right.

Chapter Twenty-Two

Malcolm, Tracey, and Joey sat in the waiting area of the hospital for the next forty-five minutes. Joey seemed twitchy and kept saying he thought maybe he should bum a cigarette from one of the nurses. "Usually, people who work in healthcare smoke," he explained. Neither Malcolm nor Tracey cared to respond to that. Tracey drank too much water and wandered in and out of the bathroom as a way to pass the time. Those forty-five minutes were the longest of her life.

Just before the doctor came to speak to Tracey, Joey pointed his water bottle from Tracey to Malcolm and back again.

"So, you guys are...?"

Tracey's lips parted in surprise. *What kind of question was that?*

"Friends," Malcolm replied firmly.

Tracey's heart pattered. *Were they friends?* They'd hardly had more than a few interactions.

Joey nodded, impressed. "I didn't know you knew any other pilots."

Tracey wanted to brag that Malcolm was actually a film director. It was petty. She kept her lips shut.

The doctor was five-foot-five with large hands and thick, horn-rimmed glasses. Tracey walked alongside him in the whitewashed hallways with her heart pressing against her ribcage.

"Mrs. Swartz, it was touch and go there for a little while, but we were able to stabilize your daughter and her pregnancy," the doctor told her.

Tracey, a woman who had never been close to being a "Mrs.", nearly sobbed with joy. "Oh my God," she whispered. "Thank you. Thank you so much."

The doctor arched an eyebrow. "We're not out of the woods quite yet. Your daughter needs hydration, good and healthy food, and plenty of rest. She also doesn't need any stress at all, certainly not the stress that comes with flying on a private plane."

He said it as though he'd seen one too many accidents in the private flying world. Tracey's hands became fists.

"I understand. She won't be in the air any time soon. I can promise you that."

Tracey sat in the chair directly beside Emma's bed and watched as her perfect, doll-like daughter slept, her hands loose across the hospital blanket and her hair shiny and clean across the pillow. In Emma's body, Tracey's grandbaby continued to grow. Tracey felt a wave of anger toward herself for having brought Joey back into their lives. *Why had she written him back in the first place?* It had been like playing with fire.

Maybe Tracey had gotten what she deserved.

Or maybe nobody ever got what they "deserved." Maybe karma wasn't real. Maybe we all just did the best we could with the information we were given. Maybe everyone did everything out of some crazy desire to love and be loved.

For the first time in a long time, Tracey noticed what time it was. She was surprised to see it was only seven at night. The day had seemed unending. The doctor had told her that Emma would probably sleep through the night. Tracey had pledged to herself that she would remain at Emma's side throughout the night, just as her mother, Mandy, had done with Alex.

Time had a way of repeating itself. And mothers had a way of always picking up the pieces.

A little while later, Tracey stood, watched her daughter from the door for another five minutes, and then convinced herself to go to the bathroom. She wandered down the hallway with her empty water bottle, blinking through the overwhelmingly sharp light.

Malcolm sat with his long legs stretched out in front of him and his head leaned against the back of the chair. He didn't look bored, far from it. It took a minute for Tracey to realize that he listened to headphones, which he popped out of his ears the minute he saw her.

"Tracey! How is she?" He stood up to his impressive height.

Tracey scanned the rest of the waiting room, which had grown emptier over the past hour. "Where's Joey?"

Malcolm grimaced. His eyes dropped to the ground. "He um. He said he had to get back to Nashville."

A stone dropped into the base of Tracey's stomach. Slowly, she knelt on a plastic chair and studied her hands. The image of herself and Joey on the beach as twenty-somethings returned to her mind. It all hadn't mattered at all, had it?

"I see." She swallowed. "Did he say anything else?"

Malcolm sat across from her. His eyes were like a puppy dog, without the hardness they usually had on set. "I don't know if I should tell you this."

"I can take anything at this point."

"He cried for a while."

Tracey's eyes widened. "You're kidding."

Malcolm rubbed the back of his hand against his chin. "Yeah. He cried hard and said he shouldn't be here anymore. That he um..." He scrunched his nose. "That he had to get back to his wife and his children."

Tracey was flabbergasted. "Wow."

"Yeah."

For a long and horrible moment, Tracey thought she would begin to sob. She thought she would have a borderline breakdown right there in the near-empty Marquette Hospital. Tears sprung to her eyes, and her throat tightened again, so hard that she thought she couldn't breathe.

Malcolm leaped to the seat beside her and placed a sturdy hand on her upper back. "Just breathe with me, okay?"

Tracey blinked several times and nodded. "Okay."

Malcolm inhaled all the air into his lungs. He then exhaled. "Slow and steady," he instructed.

It took a little while for Tracey to get the hang of breathing like him. She felt like a little kid who had to learn how to ride a bike. But finally, as the air filled her lungs and retreated out of her mouth, she found a way to feel stable again. She found a way to lift the corners of her lips.

A full ten minutes later, she whispered and said, "I was very stupid to trust him."

Malcolm just shook his head. "There's no stupidity in trusting someone. It comes from a place of love."

Tracey's nostrils flared. "I shouldn't have let him back into our lives. That's for sure."

Malcolm didn't know enough of the story to respond. All he could do was shake his head and smooth her hair. This, the act of the hair-smoothing, was proof, yet again, that Malcolm was a good father. He wouldn't have left his daughter at the hospital, struggling to keep her pregnancy viable.

"Listen," Malcolm began softly.

"Oh, goodness me," Tracey said hurriedly. "You have to go, don't you? You really should. I know that you're filming tomorrow. I don't want to take up any more of the film's time than I already have."

Malcolm's smile was soft and serene. "I do have to fly back tonight, yes. But I wondered if you'd like to grab something to eat tonight before I head out. I know it's a lot to ask since you want to sit with her while she sleeps. But..."

Tracey's eyes dampened. "I won't go anywhere but the cafeteria. But now that I'm not as terrified as I was, I'm starving."

"I'm starving, too. Let's go see if this hospital cafeteria has any Michelin Stars, shall we?"

Tracey's laughter bubbled down the hallway.

* * *

The cafeteria worker behind the counter gave them a bored, glazed smile as they entered. The specials were written on a blackboard, advertising cheeseburgers, chicken tenders, a Cobb salad, and a bowl of potato soup.

"Healthy," Malcolm muttered just loud enough for Tracey to hear.

"Yes." Tracey laughed. She couldn't have cared less. "I'll take a cheeseburger with all the fixings. Oh, and do you have fries?"

The worker nodded and placed a hamburger patty on the grill. "And you?"

"I'll have the same," Malcolm replied. "And a Diet Coke."

They sat at the corner table with their plastic trays between them. Each cheeseburger was stacked tall, with cheese oozing along the meat and buns. Tracey lifted a French fry, stabbed it in some ketchup, and ate slowly. The taste wasn't extraordinary; it was very much like a recently frozen potato that had just met its end in a greasy deep fryer. But it would do.

"My ex-wife would faint if she saw me eating this," Malcolm confessed as he wrapped his hands around the burger and lifted it to his mouth. Several pickles fell down, splattering mustard across his napkin.

Tracey laughed. "Why's that?"

"I don't think that woman has ever gone a day without eating a salad," Malcolm said. He then took a large bite, his eyes closed. Ketchup traced his lower lip and chin. After he swallowed, he said, "That is delicious."

Tracey took a bite and wanted to tell him how much better the burgers she normally made were. *But was that too presumptuous?*

"I take it your daughter isn't allowed to eat any fun, kid foods," Tracey continued, remembering the dresses. "I think my daughter lived on chicken nuggets and apple slices for an entire year. She was so picky! I couldn't get her to eat anything else."

Malcolm's eyes hardened. He took another bite and then placed his burger back on the tray. He did his best to clean himself of condiments, tearing the napkin across his fingers.

"I used to let her have treats here and there," he began. "A spoonful of ice cream or a little piece of cinnamon roll. My ex-wife eventually used that to blame me for what happened later."

Tracey placed her burger on the tray. Her pulse seemed overly loud, pounding in her ear. "What happened?"

Malcolm scratched his eyebrow. "My daughter's five. She was born healthy and happy. Ten fingers, ten toes. All signs pointed to a bright future. But about two and a half years ago, we noticed there was something wrong. She didn't immediately react to us when we spoke to her. We ignored it for a little while, but eventually, it got to the point that we had to take her in. The doctor told us that by the time she turned three, she would be completely deaf."

"Oh my God." Tracey couldn't imagine the horror of this. "And that was when you took a leave from work."

"Not right away, unfortunately, which made me feel very disconnected from the situation. My ex-wife and I fought nonstop about what to do. My thought was, you know, I'd made all this money in the film industry. It made sense that we use that money to buy our daughter implants. But my ex-wife was resistant. She threw herself completely into the world of deaf culture and began to learn sign language. I hate to say that this angered me. I just wanted to pay someone to make everything normal again. And I wanted to keep building my film career. Nothing else mattered."

Tracey nodded. She could feel the weight of his guilt.

"Eventually, my ex-wife agreed that ear implants were worth a shot. I was so happy that day. So sure that everything would be fixed. But unfortunately, the ear plants didn't take it. Our daughter screamed and cried. It was like physical pain for her. I dropped out of the project I was working on and committed to stay home full-time to help out. By then, my marriage was completely destroyed."

A tear rained down Tracey's cheek. "How is your sign language?"

Malcolm lifted his hands and, with studied precision, created images with his fingers. It looked exactly the way it did on television.

"What did you say?" Tracey asked.

"I said, 'My sign language is fine. But not as good as my ex-wife's."

"It'll take time," Tracey breathed.

Malcolm nodded. "That's what they tell me." He sipped his Diet Coke. "Things are a lot better. She's about to start at a deaf school in LA. She has deaf friends and is involved in the deaf community. For the most part, she seems to like me and wants me around. And for now, she still retains use of her voice, although I know it must feel useless for her sometimes." He swiped a tear from his cheek and added, "I love hearing that voice. It reminds me of when she first learned to speak. How exciting that was! I couldn't wait to hear all her innermost thoughts and creative ideas. Now..."

Tracey reached across their trays and wrapped a hand over Malcolm's wrist. "Now, she'll tell them to you just the same. In her own way."

Malcolm sniffed. "I hope you're right."

Tracey's heart swelled. "You're a real father, Malcolm. Emma never had one. There's a hole in her heart and her life, one that Joey should have filled. Even now, faced with the opportunity to be with her, he ran the other way."

Malcolm looked unsure. Tracey gave his wrist slightly more pressure. Their eyes connected, earnest and filled with sorrow and love.

"I'm doing the best I can," Malcolm said finally. "But it took me a long time to get to that point."

They continued to eat. Tracey was surprised at the ease with which she spoke to this hot-shot director, who, she was surprised to find out, was quite funny, as well. She laughed frequently, grateful to put her anxious thoughts somewhere else. When they scraped the last French fry through the ketchup and tossed the trash in the nearby can, they shared a hug, both with their eyes closed. Tracey was reminded of the concept of "kindred spirits." She hadn't met so many over the years. In a surprise twist, a top film director from Hollywood had become one of hers.

Chapter Twenty-Three

Tracey wasn't in any hurry to drive Emma home. In the rental vehicle, Emma was spread out in the backseat with her head propped up on a pillow and her feet up near the window. At various times, she teased Tracey, "If we drive any slower, we'll be going backwards." To this, Tracey just said, "Ha. Ha."

It was two days after the flight incident, a Sunday. The hospital had released Emma the day before, and Tracey had rented a little water-side motel room, where the two of them had sat on the cement patio— Emma technically "lying" across a flattened beach chair— and watched the lake water lap across the shore.

"I wish everyone didn't make such a fuss about this," Emma groaned as Tracey eased to a halt outside an Upper Peninsula gas station.

Tracey turned and gave her daughter her sassiest look. "Honey. Think about what you just said, and then ask yourself if it makes any gosh-darn sense."

Emma stuck out her tongue playfully. Sometimes, she still

resembled her teenage self, which was the last stronghold Tracey had to another, simpler time.

Tracey waited in line at the cash register inside the gas station, counting out bills to pay for a bag of peanuts, two bananas, and Fiji waters. Had this been another year, or even just a few months ago, she and Emma would have gorged themselves on Twizzlers and M&Ms. Just before she reached the counter, she grabbed a child-sized M&M packet, scrunching her nose. Maybe a couple of chocolates wouldn't hurt. Life was about balance, wasn't it?

Tracey prepaid for gas and lodged the gas nozzle into the side of the rental. Inside the vehicle, Emma spoke on the phone.

"I mean, it wasn't such a surprise that he left. You should have seen this guy, Meg. So charismatic. Like Grant, in a way. He promised you the world one minute and then pretended like he hardly knew you the next."

Tracey's stomach curdled. She felt terribly foolish, thinking about the love she'd once had for Joey and just how wrong everything had gone.

The gas rushed through the tube and filled the tank, and the air stank and thickened. Inside the car, Emma continued, "Yeah. Handsome pilot. Thought he knew everything about everything. But when I came up to him in the plane and said, 'Um, Joey, I'm bleeding,' he looked like he'd seen a ghost. All the color drained from his face. That's when I knew he was panicking."

When Emma had awoken Saturday morning after her long sleep, she'd taken one look at Tracey and said, "He left, didn't he?" When Tracey had told her, "Yes, baby. He did." Emma had shaken her head and said, "We never needed him. Not then, and not now." Tracey had known not to talk about it again.

It was like Joey had died.

It was better this way.

* * *

Tracey rented a wheelchair from the ferry company; because she was an islander with a necessary need, the ferry company waived all fees. She then wheeled her daughter up from the ferry docks back toward home. Emma grumbled that she felt "stupid, foolish, and lazy." When they passed The Grind, the coffee shop managed by Wayne and her cousin, Michael, Wayne caught sight of them and hopped out, waving a hand. His eyes were wide and panicked.

"Hi there," he said, continuously drying his already-dry hands across his apron. "Glad to see you two made it back."

Emma groaned. "You don't have to feel sorry for me."

Wayne laughed. "We were just worried, Em. You can't blame us."

"No more worrying allowed," Emma told him. "I'm fine. My baby's fine. The only one we need to watch out for around here is..." She pointed her thumb back toward Tracey.

Wayne's smile widened. "I don't know about that. Your mother is quite a trooper."

"She drove me home at five miles per hour," Emma explained.

"Safety first," Tracey explained.

When they reached the front porch of Tracey's house, Tracey blinked at the ominous staircase in front of them— no more than four steps, yet basically a mountain.

"Mom, I can walk a few steps," Emma said, reading her mother's mind.

Suddenly, the front door screamed open. Megan appeared over the railing of the porch, grinning madly.

Emma shrieked with surprise. "What the heck are you doing here?"

"I leave you for one week, Emma. One week! And you wind up in the hospital?" Megan took a step down the porch staircase as the screen door flailed open again to reveal Cindy, followed by Elise.

"I was literally just talking to you on the phone," Emma shot out. "You lied that you were going out to get bagels in East Lansing!"

"Oh. Yeah. I did that on the way to grab the bus this morning," Megan said, waving her hand. She rushed down and wrapped her arms around her cousin, her face scrunching and turning tomato-red.

Tracey wanted to point out that it was their family's right to be terrified for Emma and to love her to bits. But she figured Megan, Cindy, and Elise's surprise attack at the house was proof enough.

Tracey and Megan helped Emma step gingerly up the staircase. Elise hurriedly opened a beach chair so that Emma could lay back on it. Cindy disappeared into the house and returned with a fresh strawberry cake covered with low-fat whipped cream. All three of them beamed at Emma continually, overcompensating for their own fear.

"I feel like the Queen of England," Emma announced.

Cindy sat at the porch table and heaved a sigh. "Two pregnant women in the family! How did we get so lucky?"

"How is Margot doing?" Emma asked. She placed her hand easily over her stomach, claiming her status as a "mother." It wasn't a secret any longer.

"She says she's about as big as a whale," Cindy explained. "It should be any day now. Michael looks white as a sheet."

"We'll raise our babies together," Emma said wistfully.

Cindy's eyes watered. She grabbed a napkin and tapped beneath them, catching tears. Elise demanded the full story of what had happened, which led Emma to explain, point-blank, that, "The director of your film flew Mom all the way to Marquette in his private jet."

Tracey had purposefully left this element of the story out of her text messages and phone calls. Elise, Cindy, and Megan's jaws dropped.

"Malcolm?" Elise gasped.

"It wasn't a private jet," Tracey tried to explain. She needed them to know it wasn't that big of a deal. "Like, not the way you see on those TV shows, with the gold-plated everything and the faucets with champagne instead of water. It was a two-seater plane."

"Mom. A famous film director stopped the filming of his movie to fly you to see me," Emma said firmly. "Just accept that it's a special story. Just accept that that actually happened."

Tracey's stomach tightened. She wasn't sure where to put her hands. Elise exhaled all the air from her lungs and whispered, "Sometimes, people surprise you."

"Malcolm is maybe the most surprising man I've ever met," Tracey admitted, mostly to her toes.

Megan and Cindy exchanged glances. A breeze shifted across the porch, tinged with a chill. It was August, but so far north, late summer reminded you that you were never far from the approaching darkness.

Cindy cut the cake, taking on the role of the matriarch. She could have been Mandy before her. Tracey traced the tongs of her fork over the whipped cream, listening to Emma tell a story about the hospital nurse who'd asked her if she was ready for "surgery" and begun to prepare to wheel her bed out of the room. Emma and Tracey had popped up, crying, "You have the wrong room!"

Tracey chewed the strawberry cake slowly, rolling the sweetness over her tongue. Her phone buzzed in her purse, and she searched for it, half-hoping that it was Joey, explaining himself. But instead, it was that remarkable man, Malcolm. A hero in every sense.

MALCOLM: I hope you made it back, okay?

MALCOLM: It's hard to believe we're so close to finishing the on-island filming.

MALCOLM: This summer has been such a strange one.

MALCOLM: I'm glad you were a part of it.

Tracey blinked back tears and shoved her phone back into her pocket. She heard herself respond to a question from Cindy; she even made a joke, which she immediately forgot. All the while, she felt her heart face a difficult realization— one that had been lurking within her since her conversation with Malcolm.

No matter how much of an understanding they had, their friendship (or whatever it was) couldn't go forward. Not in any real way.

Malcolm's world existed in Los Angeles, where he would do everything he could for his daughter.

And Tracey's was there, on Mackinac Island, with Emma and her new grandchild.

"Would you like another slice?" Cindy asked Tracey, dragging her out of her reverie.

Tracey nodded, blinking back tears. She felt heavy with a mix of nostalgia and hope. Even the recipe reminded her of long-ago afternoons in her youth.

"I'd like that very much," she told her sister. "Thank you."

Chapter Twenty-Four

At five-thirty in the morning on Friday, August 12th, Tracey sat at the far end of the ferry docks with her bare feet hanging toward the water. She still wore her running clothes, and they were slick with sweat and heavy against her skin. Out in the distance, a sailboat championed across the horizon line. *Who sailed so early in the morning?* Tracey wondered. But almost immediately, the answer came to her— those who braved the early morning were allowed a heavenly portrait of a brand-new day. It was certainly why she loved her morning runs.

"Look what the cat dragged out here." A voice rang out behind Tracey.

Tracey turned to watch Marcy with a mug of coffee lifted. Her long runner's legs strode out before her, muscular and easy.

"Marcy! Aren't you a sight for sore eyes? Did you already finish your run?"

Marcy stopped about five feet from Tracey, sipped her

coffee with her eyes closed, and then fluttered her fingers across the edge of her runner's shorts. "There's something about today. Something that makes me want to sit still."

Tracey swallowed the lump in her throat. The morning when Marcy had discovered Tracey and Cindy naked in the waters off the ferry dock felt like three years ago. *Had it actually been just over six weeks?*

Summer had a way of playing around with time. Tracey knew that.

"Care if I sit?" Marcy asked. Without pausing for an answer, she crouched and dropped her feet over the water, careful not to spill a single drop of coffee.

Together, Marcy and Tracey held the silence for a long time, their eyes on the horizon and the dock creaking gently beneath them.

"That Joey was never right for you," Marcy said suddenly, apropos of nothing.

Tracey dropped her chin to her chest. As the island bartender, Marcy had a way with people and a clear understanding of what made them tick. Probably, she'd taken one look at Joey all those years ago and thought, "What a rascal." All Tracey had been able to do at the time was fall in love.

Tracey lifted her shoulders evenly. "I guess you heard what happened."

"Darling, you know it doesn't take a lot for an old gossip like me to hear what's what," Marcy said. Her eyes glittered knowingly as she took another sip of coffee. "Rumor has it that director has an eye for you, though."

Tracey's cheeks burned. In the distance, the same sailboat seemed to sail backward, heading back to wherever it had come from.

"He has a life out in Los Angeles," Tracey told her softly. "Whatever there was between us, it's just a fantasy."

"And thank God for fantasies," Marcy said with finality. "Life would be a whole lot more boring without them."

* * *

It was the final day of filming. After that weekend, Malcolm, Donna, the cast, and much of the crew would return to Los Angeles, where they would film the rest of what was needed in sound stages and studios. Every task Tracey performed over that morning and afternoon felt heavy with nostalgia. There were final pins to slide into fabrics; there were final pant legs to roll up. There were final laughs to have with particularly silly extras, some she'd grown to love over the previous month.

Toward the tail-end of the day, Donna put Tracey in charge of the costuming for the main actress. Donna had selected most of the outfits already, but told Tracey to "follow her heart" when it came to accessories. Tracey selected a beautiful, pearl-lined barrette and a thin necklace with a heavy, old-fashioned pendant. Each contrasted with the otherwise light and trendy summer dress that the main actress wore. This, Tracey felt, called back to the "seventies" era of the film— uniting the past story and the present story with symbols.

What Tracey did wasn't lost on Donna. "It's perfect," she said, cocking her head. "I would have gone a different direction, one that wouldn't have served the scene as well." She then gripped Tracey's shoulder as she asked, yet again, "Why don't you come out to Los Angeles with us? We could really use your eye."

But again, Tracey gave Donna a gracious smile. "I have to stay here. Emma's here. My family's here."

Donna, who'd probably made every decision in her life with her career in mind, simply nodded. "I wish I could understand you," she said. "But perhaps it's better that I can't."

* * *

They returned to the beach for the final scene. An orange bulb of a sun dunked across the Straits of Mackinac and cast everything in a nostalgic light. Malcolm, behind the camera, called out that they had to act quickly. "The light is perfect right now. Just perfect. I don't want to waste it."

Tracey rushed into the shot to fix the way the main actress's dress hung across her legs. When she fled back, she locked eyes once more with Malcolm, who nodded and gave her a soft smile. Her heart cracked at the edges.

Tracey hadn't told anyone about the past week and a half—about Malcolm and Tracey's long walks along the water, about the fact that they'd already told one another the innermost secrets of their hearts, and about one particularly romantic night that she'd prayed would never end.

That night had ended. It had. Tracey had eventually washed her face and applied her retinol. She'd eventually turned out all her lights and walked past the room where Emma now slept full-time as they'd moved her out of the apartment over the fudge shop. She'd then tucked herself into bed and told herself not to dream of him. It hadn't worked.

"CUT!" Malcolm cried after the final take. He smacked his palms together and said, "Everyone, give yourselves a round of applause. Fantastic work. Really. Just fantastic."

A stereo system began to blare "Take The Long Way Home" by Supertramp. Suddenly, arms were flung around Tracey's frame. She recognized Donna's perfume and turned to find Donna half-sobbing, trying to compose herself.

"Thank you for everything," Donna told her. "You really held me together during this shoot." She swiped her hand under her eye, collecting tears. "I just hope that we can remain friends."

Tracey, who hadn't ever considered Donna a friend, just

nodded, smiled, and hugged Donna back. "We'll stay friends. I promise."

As the film equipment was moved to the side and organized in trailers, several food truck trailers arrived, advertising sandwiches, burritos, pizzas, and sushi. Several bars were set up along the beach. Already, handsome bartenders shook shakers filled with cocktails and chatted to film workers who looked eager for a drink. Tracey and Donna walked up to the closest bar and ordered two margaritas lined with thick shards of salt. They clinked the sides of their glasses carefully, sharing a moment of quiet exhaustion.

"Malcolm won't know what to do without you," Donna said softly, watching as Malcolm walked across the sand, chatting with one of the assistant directors. His smile was confident, clear.

"He will. He already does," Tracey breathed. She took another sip of the tangy margarita, fluttering her eyes closed. When she opened them again, she found Malcolm peering back at her, a drink lifted. She lifted hers in return.

"The studio was up in arms when they heard that Malcolm shut down the shoot to take you up to Marquette," Donna explained under her breath.

"Were they?" Malcolm hadn't told her anything about that.

"Malcolm shut them down," Donna explained. "He said there was a family emergency. They couldn't figure out how to attack him for that." Donna placed one of her sharp elbows on Tracey's upper arm and said, "That's the kind of power you have, Trace. An entire film shut down production for you. A powerful man is falling in love with you. And you have the strength to turn your back on all of it. I can't tell if you're a genius or the craziest woman in the world."

Tracey laughed, her stomach tightening. "I'll keep you updated on that."

Elise, Wayne, Penny, Cindy, Ron, Michael, Emma, and

Dean arrived a little while later. They'd taken a glossy carriage like tourists. Dean sat directly behind the two horses, directing them to the beach. He beamed with pride.

Emma walked daintily through the sand, her hand on her stomach. Tracey hugged her tenderly as a single tear fell down her cheek. The doctor had given her the all-clear on getting back to her life. It was marvelous to see her back at the beach, her eyes catching the last light of the gorgeous summer evening.

Elise hugged Tracey next, chatting about her next trip to Los Angeles and Penny's decision to return to California.

"I've had a great summer," Penny explained. "But I let a Michigan boy break my heart. It's time for me to get out of here."

"It happens to the best of us," Emma said coaxingly.

"It's okay. I have a lot of material to draw from for my next acting course," Penny said.

"I wish I could use my ex for something like that," Emma tried.

"Why can't you?" Penny asked with a shrug. "Come on. Just because you're pregnant doesn't mean you shouldn't be making art all of the time. Write a poem about how much you hate him! Tell a story about the island! Bring us into that world of yours!" Penny shook her head wildly, as though she couldn't wrap her mind around being passive at any moment.

There was a light in Emma's eyes, proof that she understood. Just because Megan had run off to build her own life in East Lansing didn't mean Emma couldn't find her own truth. "Maybe I will," she told Penny.

A little while later, Penny and Emma bobbed gently to the stereo beats on the dance floor. One of the twenty-something male extras chatted up Emma, wearing an overwhelmed smile. Tracey sipped her margarita, wondering what on earth would happen next.

And as though she'd called to him, he appeared beside her.

"Not a bad party," Malcolm said, his hand on her upper arm.

She shivered with longing, which she soon shoved away. "Mackinac has a way of pulling out some delicious summer nights. I see that she served us well tonight."

Malcolm laughed and sipped his craft beer. His eyes were contented.

"You must be happy to get back to see your daughter," Tracey said softly. Her voice broke slightly, betraying her.

Malcolm's cheek twitched. "I'm looking forward to it. Apparently, she's already torn a hole in one of the dresses I got her from your shop."

Tracey's laughter sparkled. "That's what kids are supposed to do. Break things. Grow out of things. Make messes. It's probably foolish of us to try to put them in pretty dresses. They're just going to live in them and live well."

Malcolm's smile lifted. "I had that same thought. And you know what? It pleased me to no end, knowing that just because she can't hear anymore doesn't mean she isn't just a little kid. A little kid who will get into trouble. A little kid who will get angry with her parents. A little kid with big emotions."

Tracey, who currently felt like a big kid with big emotions, took another sip of her second margarita.

There was a long moment of silence. Tracey's heart pounded. She had to tell him what was heavy on her mind. After the party, it would be too late.

"Before this summer, I didn't think I was worthy of... much of anything," Tracey began.

"Tracey—" Malcolm tried to interrupt.

"No, don't." She swallowed. "I didn't think I would be any good at this movie stuff. I didn't think I was good enough to date or want more out of my life than what I already had. In some ways, I thought that living for the boutique and for my family was enough. Maybe it was, for a long time. But now that I've had more, now that I've felt more, I know that there's a whole lot more living out there for me. And gosh, I'm so grateful for that. And for you, for showing me that."

Malcolm's eyes closed for a long time. He dropped his shoulders forward.

"I think people come into our lives for a reason," Tracey continued, her voice raspy. "You came into mine when I needed you the most. And just because our time together is over doesn't mean I won't always treasure it. I will. With everything I am."

Malcolm reached out and laced his fingers through hers. His eyes were steady. She could have held his gaze for another hour longer.

"I will always treasure it," Malcolm echoed her words. "And I know we'll see one another again, somewhere along the way."

Soon after, one of the assistant directors hustled up to ask Malcolm a question. Malcolm walked off with him, moving his free hand through the air to solidify his point. For a strange moment, Tracey felt terribly alone, with the sharp chill of the lake digging into her bones.

"There she is. My big-time Hollywood celebrity." Tracey's father, Dean Swartz, appeared beside her. As ever, he wore a plaid shirt and a pair of jeans and, despite the incredible selection of beer, wine, and cocktails, had stuck to domestic beer.

"Hi, Dad." Tracey thought her heart might shatter. She told herself to keep it together in front of her father.

He sipped his domestic beer and watched the large bonfire as it flickered and spat toward the sky. "Some party," he said.

"Some party," she agreed.

Dean's eyes reflected everything that he knew— that Joey had come back into their lives, only to flee again; that Emma had been hospitalized and had eventually moved in with Tracey; that Tracey refused a future in Los Angeles, all for the love of her family.

"I just wanted to tell you how proud I am to know you," Dean told her softly. "Not only as my daughter, who I love. But as a woman of Mackinac Island, a place where family is held above everything else. Your mother was there in that hospital room with you that night. She sees the sacrifices you're making. And she loves you for them."

Tracey's eyes filled with tears. She dropped her head against her father's upper arm and told herself to keep it together. In the distance, someone popped a bottle of champagne, and the sound rocketed up through the cliffside and the nearby forest. Tracey felt utterly wordless.

"Mom! Come make a s'more with me!" Emma appeared before them with two sticks. She slid marshmallows along the end and passed the stick over to Tracey, just as she had when she was eight or nine or ten. Tracey followed after her and placed the marshmallow an inch or so from the flickering flames.

Emma's lips curved into a gorgeous smile as she watched the marshmallow roasting to a perfect tan. Tracey couldn't help but watch her daughter, thinking about the millions of tiny moments just like this. As a single mother, those moments had all belonged to her and her alone. *How lucky she was.*

"Mom! Your marshmallow!" Emma cried.

Distracted, Tracey had allowed hers to burn to a black char. Tracey waved a hand and said, "It's okay. Sometimes, they're better this way." She then removed the blackened mallow and stuck it in her mouth, her eyes closed as the sweet goop coursed over her tongue. Emma laughed joyously and tossed her head back, her eyes toward the sky.

Very soon, they would teach Emma's baby to live just like

this— to appreciate gorgeous summers on Mackinac, where bonfires burned late into the night, and there were always enough s'mores to go around.

It was the Michigan way.

Next in the Secrets of Mackinac Island

The Mackinac Bride

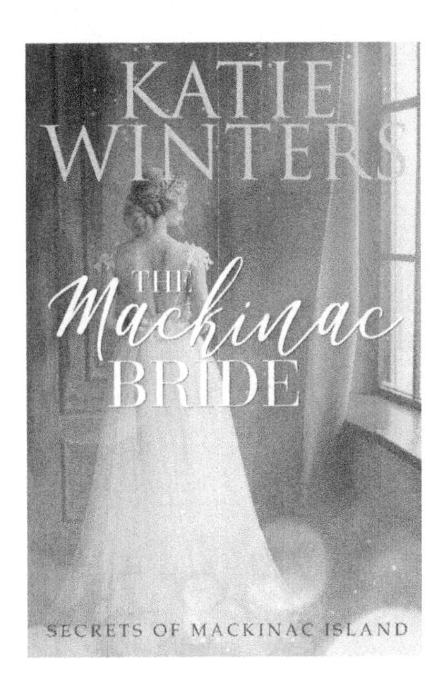

Other Books by Katie

The Vineyard Sunset Series

Secrets of Mackinac Island Series

Sisters of Edgartown Series

A Katama Bay Series

A Mount Desert Island Series

Connect with Katie Winters

BookBub
Facebook
Newsletter

To receive exclusive updates from Katie Winters please sign up to be on her Newsletter!
CLICK HERE TO SUBSCRIBE

Made in the USA
Monee, IL
11 January 2023